Tunde and the Leopard-Man. *Page 50.*

AJAPA THE TORTOISE
A BOOK OF NIGERIAN FOLK TALES

MARGARET BAUMANN

WITH THE ORIGINAL ILLUSTRATIONS BY
G. R. DAY

DOVER PUBLICATIONS, INC.
MINEOLA, NEW YORK

This book is dedicated
to
Layinka and Derek
and to
a funny little person, the hero—and sometimes
the villain—of many Nigerian stories, and the friend
of all Nigerian children,

AJAPA THE TORTOISE

Bibliographical Note

This Dover edition, first published in 2002, is an unabridged republication of the edition published by A. & C. Black, Ltd., London, in 1929. The eight full-page illustrations by G. R. Day, originally in color, are reproduced here in black and white.

Library of Congress Cataloging-in-Publication Data

Baumann, Margaret.
    Ajapa the tortoise : a book of Nigerian folk tales / Margaret Baumann.
       p. cm.
    Originally published: London : A. & C. Black, 1929.
    Summary: A collection of thirty folk tales which feature the trickster, Tortoise, and other jungle animals.
    ISBN-13: 978-0-486-42361-6
    ISBN-10: 0-486-42361-1
    1. Tales—Nigeria. [1. Folklore—Nigeria. 2. Turtles—Folklore.] I. Title.

PZ8.1.B344 Aj 2002
398.2—dc21

2002073996

Manufactured in the United States by RR Donnelley
42361103   2015
www.doverpublications.com

Contents

Illustrations

I. Tortoise Goes Wooing

Tortoise and Pigeon were great friends. One day Tortoise came to Pigeon and said:

"Pigeon, I have fallen in love with a charming maiden named Nyanribo. She lives a good distance from here, but I am going to visit her to-morrow, and I would like you to accompany me."

"With pleasure!" agreed Pigeon; and early next morning they set out.

As they journeyed, Tortoise spent the time describing the charms of his lady-love—her beauty, her elegance, her wit and generosity—until Pigeon began to think she must be the most perfect tortoise in the world.

"Of course she is!" said Tortoise. "That is why I love her. You will see how pleased she is to see me to-day, but it is a pity she lives in such a remote place."

"It is indeed," replied his friend, who began to feel very tired of walking.

Soon afterwards they came to a country that was very rough and stony.

"Alas!" said Tortoise. "It will take me at least two days to walk across this stony ground. Will you not fly with me on your back until we reach a better country for walking?"

Pigeon kindly agreed to carry his friend, and flew with him for a considerable distance, until they saw smooth fields beneath them.

"Now you can walk again," said Pigeon, flying down to the ground.

They had not gone far when they came to a wide river.

1

"Now," cried Tortoise, "how in the world are we to cross this river, unless you carry me again?"

"I am very tired!" murmured Pigeon; but Tortoise pretended not to hear, and climbed on to his back.

Pigeon flew across the wide river and came down to earth on the other side. But Tortoise refused to dismount.

"You carry me so awkwardly," he said, "that I have terrible cramp and could not possibly walk. You will have to fly the rest of the way."

So poor Pigeon carried him all the way to Nyanribo's house. Now the house consisted of two rooms, and Tortoise left Pigeon in the outer room while he entered the inner room to see his lady-love.

He found Nyanribo waiting with a splendid banquet spread ready. She had prepared so many good things to eat and drink that there was enough for a large family.

"Where is your friend Pigeon?" asked Nyanribo.

"Oh," said Tortoise, "my friend is a funny bird. He is so shy that if you speak to him he will die of fright, and he wishes to remain in the outer room until it is time to depart. Now let us enjoy the dinner you have prepared."

They began to eat, while poor Pigeon waited hungry and thirsty in the other room.

When he had nearly finished all that was on the table, Tortoise said:

"I can see you are a good cook, and I love you very much. Will you be my wife?"

"Yes," said Nyanribo. "If I did not mean to be your wife, I should not have taken so much trouble preparing a feast for you. But I am worried about your friend Pigeon. What will he have to eat?"

"I told you," replied Tortoise, "that my friend is a very strange bird. He never eats when he is away from home, and the only thing he will not refuse is a bowl of water."

Nyanribo at once filled a bowl with fresh water, and Tortoise carried it to his friend in the other room.

"My poor friend," he said, looking very mournful, "Nyanribo mistook the day of our visit, and as she did not expect us until to-morrow, she has nothing in the house to eat, but she sends you this bowl of water. She has been making apologies to me all this while."

Tortoise then quickly returned to the inner room to finish what remained of the feast. Pigeon waited for some time, and then grew so impatient that he could not help peeping into the other room.

There he saw Tortoise and Nyanribo talking and looking well-fed and comfortable, while on the ground were a great number of empty dishes. Seeing this, Pigeon understood the trick which Tortoise had played on him, and went back to the outer room to plan his revenge.

At last Tortoise came to him and said that it was time to depart. They travelled slowly homewards until they reached the wide river.

"You will carry me, dear Pigeon, will you not?" said Tortoise, who had eaten so much that he could hardly walk at all.

"Certainly, dear Tortoise," replied Pigeon, "but I do not wish you to have cramp again, so I will hold one of your feet in my beak instead of carrying you on my back."

When they were half-way across the river, Pigeon dropped Tortoise into the water and flew away.

When he had flown for some time, he saw in the field below him a dead horse, and quickly thought of another trick to play Tortoise, if he managed to escape from the river. He went to a man who lived near by, and asked him to cut off the horse's head, which he then arranged on the ground, and, flying up into a tree, he prepared to watch what might happen.

Now when Pigeon let Tortoise drop from his beak, he did not fall into the river, where he would certainly have been drowned, but on to the back of a hippopotamus which was just swimming to the bank. As the big animal reached the bank, Tortoise climbed off its back and hurried away as fast as he could.

Later on he came to a field where there was a horse's head standing on the ground. Tortoise was so much astonished at seeing this marvel, that he did not go home, but went instead to the King of the country and told him that he knew of a place where horses' heads grew out of the ground just like plants.

Tortoise Finds the Horse's Head. *Page 3.*

The King was delighted, and said that if the story was true he would give Tortoise a basket full of gold, which would make him rich for life.

Tortoise agreed to take the King and all his Court to the place where horses' heads grew like plants, and they all set off, accompanied by drummers, warriors, and a great crowd of people who desired to see this astonishing thing.

But, alas! When they reached the field there was nothing to be seen, for Pigeon had removed the head.

The King was very angry, and ordered Tortoise to be burnt to death for deceiving him. Poor Tortoise pleaded in vain for pardon. The warriors made a great bonfire in the field and flung Tortoise into the flames.

Just at that moment the sky became dark with the wings of birds. Pigeon had watched everything from his perch on the tree, but when he saw that Tortoise would be killed he was sorry, and quickly summoned all the tribe of pigeons and doves to rescue his ungrateful friend. With their wings they beat out the flames, and Tortoise was saved.

Then Pigeon related the whole story to the King, and explained how he had played a trick on Tortoise with the horse's head. At this the King forgave Tortoise, and allowed the two friends to continue their journey together.

But Tortoise was overcome with shame at the thought of Pigeon's goodness after he had been so meanly treated.

"Let us return at once to Nyanribo's house," he said, "and I will order her to make an even more excellent feast, and you shall eat it all yourself."

"I will gladly come back with you," replied Pigeon, "but it would be no pleasure to me to eat the feast alone. True friends find the best enjoyment in sharing their good fortune."

"You are right," replied Tortoise, "and I am sure that when you go wooing, you will not treat your friends as badly as I have treated you!"

II. Why Women Have Long Hair

In the days when women had short hair just like men, there lived a poor widow called Bisi in a little hut in a village close to the forest.

Every evening the women of the village went in a long row, singing, through part of the forest, with water-pots on their heads, to draw water from a well some distance away. Bisi went with them, and when she returned home she would light a fire in front of her hut, put on a pot, and cook the evening meal for herself and her son.

But one evening when it was time to make the fire, she found that she had no wood. So she ran to the next hut and asked for a few sticks, but her neighbour had none to spare, and, in fact, though she asked in every hut, nobody could give her wood to make a fire.

"Well," said Bisi, "I shall have to go to the forest and cut some wood myself, because my son is away."

She took an axe and went into the forest, but she was very angry at having to waste so much time just when she should have been preparing the meal.

The first tree she came to was the Iroko, which is a magic tree and must never be cut down.

"I don't care," thought Bisi. "I will cut off these low branches and chop them into sticks, so that no one will know I have touched the magic tree."

In haste she did so, and soon returned to the village, carrying a large bundle of sticks, with which she made a roaring fire and cooked a savoury stew for her supper.

Then she went to sleep and forgot all about the wood she had cut, though the wise men declare that: "He who harms the Iroko tree will meet with sorrow in return."

Next evening the women went as usual along the forest-path to the well, and Bisi went with them.

But as she passed by the Iroko tree, a hole suddenly appeared in the ground under Bisi's feet, and she felt herself falling.

"Help me! Save me!" she cried and the other women all dropped their water-pots and rushed to her, seizing hold of her by the hair just as she was disappearing.

They pulled and pulled, but Bisi continued to sink, and so her hair grew longer and longer. At last, when her hair was almost a yard long, they gave an extra hard tug, and managed to pull her up out of the hole.

Then they collected their water-pots and ran back to the village as fast as they could. Bisi ran the fastest of all, but when they questioned her, she was forced to confess that she had chopped some branches from the magic tree to make a fire.

"You have been very wicked, Bisi," said the Chief of the village, "but the Iroko has punished you sufficiently by making your hair grow so ridiculously long."

Everyone laughed at her, and for a long time she was ashamed of her long hair. But one day, looking at herself in a pool of water, she found that her hair was beautiful, so she twined flowers and ornaments into it, and was very proud, forgetting that it was a punishment.

Then the other women grew jealous, and they all wished for long hair. At last they all agreed to dig a deep hole, and each of them in turn jumped in, while the rest held her by the hair until her tresses were stretched to a great length.

In the evening they all returned to the village rejoicing, with long hair twined with flowers and gold ornaments.

And since that time all women have had long hair.

III. How Tortoise Became a Chief

Tortoise was nothing if not ambitious, and having risen from being a very insignificant creature to be known as a person of consequence, there was one honour which he greatly desired—to become a Chief.

One night he roused Nyanribo, his wife, just as she was falling asleep.

"What *is* the matter, Tortoise?" she complained. "I am too sleepy to listen to the account of any of your wonderful exploits, and I must really ask you once again to tell me your adventures at a more suitable time."

"My dear," replied Tortoise plaintively, "why do you misjudge me so rashly? I am not about to tell you of my adventures in peril and disaster; I merely wanted to say that unless I soon become a Chief I shall pine away and die. The desire fills my mind the whole time, so that I can neither eat nor sleep. I am worn to a shadow."

"You are a very thick shadow, husband!" retorted Nyanribo crossly. "How can you possibly wear the robes of a Chief on your slippery back? You will make a laughing-stock of us with your silly ambitions."

"All the same," persisted Tortoise, "I simply must become a Chief, and I shall not rest until I have found a way of gaining what I desire."

"Oh, how tiresome you are! Ask the King to make you a Chief, to be sure!" answered his wife, and fell asleep again.

Tortoise thought over her words until at last he had an idea. Then he fell asleep too.

The next day he made his way to the King's palace.

"Your Majesty," he said, jerking his head up and down in salute, "I have come to crave a favour."

"What is your request, O Tortoise?" asked the King.

"Sire," replied Tortoise, "I greatly desire to become a Chief."

At this the King and all his Court were convulsed with merriment.

"I have often heard that Tortoise is ambitious," said the King, "but I never thought he would claim a chiefdom!"

"Sire, next week a great event takes place—your birthday. If I were a Chief I should feel at liberty to present Your Majesty with the most unique gift you have ever received."

The King could not help feeling curious when Tortoise made this cunning suggestion, and asked him what was the nature of the present.

"Alas!" replied Tortoise, "I shall never have the delight of giving the present to you, so why should I arouse your curiosity by describing it? I can only say that it is absolutely unique."

The King could not bear to think of losing such a remarkable present, so he consented to make Tortoise a Chief, and the ceremony took place at once.

Tortoise went home very joyfully, and engaged ten strong labourers, who went out each day and returned at night carrying a heavy burden. This went on for several days, until the morning of the King's birthday dawned.

The King sat under a large white umbrella, and slaves fanned him with woven fans, while all the Chiefs bowed before him and brought him presents of great value. One brought ornaments of gold; another offered him an elephant's tusk carved with praises of the King; another brought a cloak made entirely of lions' manes and bordered with the skin of the rarest snakes.

Only Chief Tortoise was absent.

The King's warriors next performed a dance before him, and the agile acrobats turned somersaults to the pleasure of all beholders.

Still Tortoise was absent. The King's frown grew heavier and heavier as evening came on and no Tortoise appeared.

"If Chief Tortoise remains absent one hour longer," declared the King angrily, "it will cost him his head!"

Now the King was a rather ferocious monarch, and many heads had been sacrificed, both in peace and war, for his pleasure.

The hour passed slowly. The celebrations fell flat; the struggles of the wrestlers, the witty songs of the dancers, and the lively playing of the drummers—all failed to bring even one smile to the King's face.

Then suddenly Chief Tortoise was seen in the far distance, approaching slowly and followed by twenty tall labourers.

The drummers began to play, the dancers clapped their hands and sang:

> "Hail to Ajapa, Chief Tortoise!
> Hail! oh, hail!"

As Tortoise and his labourers approached, it was seen that Tortoise wore upon his back (which was at that time perfectly smooth and flat) a little mantle of gold cloth like a Chief, and that his twenty labourers were bowed low under the weight of large nets which they carried over their shoulders, and which seemed to be full of round, hairy objects.

The King sprang to his feet, crying:

"He has brought me a present of heads! Chief Tortoise, you are welcome. Come and sit beside me."

The twenty labourers laid down their nets some distance away, and Tortoise sat down beside the King, so that all the other Chiefs, who would have liked to sit under the white umbrella where Tortoise was, were filled with envy.

"Illustrious King," said Tortoise, "shaker of the earth, monarch of the forest, ruler of elephants and serpents, we are all assembled here to rejoice in your royal birthday, and I am glad to think that I have brought you a gift which is unique."

"Chief Tortoise," replied the King, "your present fills me with delight. I have never seen a collection of so many heads, and I am sure you must have gone through many perils and adventures to obtain them. I am not ungrateful, and I would like to hear how your present was obtained."

Tortoise cleared his throat as if he were about to tell a long story, but at that moment a certain Chief drew close to the King and cried:

"Sire, the heads which Tortoise has brought are nothing but coconuts!" And he flourished before the King's face a large and shaggy coconut.

The King rushed to the spot where the labourers had put down their nets, and found that truly the nets were filled with a grand collection of coconuts.

"So this is your unique present!" he said grimly. "At least I will have one head—your own!"

"Your Majesty," pleaded Tortoise, trembling with fear, "I crave forgiveness. I am very, very poor, as Your Majesty may perhaps remember, yet I truly desired to find a unique present, and I still claim that I have done so. I am quite convinced that Your Majesty has never before received five hundred coconuts, and if this is the case, then surely you will not desire my death, for I have done what I promised. I never said that I had brought a gift of heads."

"It is true, presumptuous Chief, that I have never received five hundred coconuts," replied the King, who could not refrain from smiling. "It is equally true that I have no use whatever for five hundred coconuts, and I therefore command you to eat them all yourself!"

All the Court rocked with merriment at this decree, but Tortoise was filled with consternation. In vain did he plead for mercy, promising to secure ten or even twelve real heads by some means or other.

The King's slaves began to open the coconuts one after another. Tortoise stood in front of the growing pile and began to eat. One coconut was quite sufficient for him, and when he had eaten three (by this time the night was far advanced) he felt extremely uncomfortable.

In the morning he was still eating, and the huge pile of coconuts was only decreased by ten. But alas for poor Tortoise! His back, which had always been so smooth and flat, was curved into the hump which his descendants still wear to-day.

Seeing his sad condition, the King relented and declared

himself satisfied. At this, Tortoise collapsed and was carried home by his labourers.

"Now you see what it means to become a Chief!" said his wife, but for once Tortoise made no reply.

In time he recovered from the ill-effects of his feast, but to this day he has no liking for coconuts.

IV. The Inquisitive Servant

There was once a poor boy called Ladipo, who had the power of changing himself into any form he desired, but so far the charm had not been of any use to him, and as he stood in the market-place one afternoon he felt hungry and miserable, for he had not a single cowrie with which to buy fried plantains or even corn.

As he leaned listlessly against a wall, he was suddenly aware that two men were talking eagerly at the other side.

"How great is the treasure?" asked the first.

"Oh, very great—a king's ransom, all in gold and ivory," replied the other. "We and our friend can share it all, since no one else knows where it is buried. We shall all three be rich for life."

By this time Ladipo was listening intently, but he very much desired to see the two speakers, so he quickly changed himself into a fly and buzzed up to the top of the wall. He saw a very fat man and a very thin one, squatting on the ground with their heads together. They were whispering now in very low tones, and in order to hear what they said the fly settled on the head of the fat man and listened.

"We will start this evening," said the fat man. "I think it will be a good idea if you can find a trustworthy servant to carry our provisions, for the journey is long, and you know the treasure lies buried in the depths of the forest. Do you agree?"

"Yes," said the thin man; "but wait a moment! There is a big fly on your head, and I am going to kill it."

But of course the fly was gone, and in his own form Ladipo

waited eagerly in the market-place until at last he saw the thin man walking about alone, buying provisions which he placed in a large basket.

Ladipo approached him and said politely:

"Sir, you appear to be getting ready for a journey. Do you by any chance require a servant? My master has just died, and I have nothing to do."

The thin man observed him carefully and replied:

"You are very small and do not appear strong."

"That," said the boy, "is because I have had nothing to eat to-day. If you will give me two plantains, you will see how briskly I can carry your basket. I am a very good cook besides."

So the thin man agreed to take him, and gave him some fruit to eat. After that Ladipo felt quite lively and excited, and stepped along so boldly with the basket on his head that the thin man was glad to have found him and quite proud when he showed him that evening to his two friends.

Ladipo, of course, recognized the fat man, and he found that the third traveller was a man with a long black beard, but they all had such strange names that the boy decided to call them simply Fat, Thin, and Beard.

The four of them set off at once and travelled for a long distance into the forest. Even when it was quite dark they did not stop, for they had a little lamp and seemed to know the way by heart. At last the servant was so tired that he felt sure he would soon go to sleep standing up.

When they had gone still further, poor Ladipo felt that he could not endure his weariness any longer, so, pretending that something had fallen out of his basket, he asked one of the travellers to carry the basket while he ran back to pick up what was lost.

"You cannot find it in the dark," said Thin.

"Oh yes, I have the eyes of a leopard!" replied the servant; and Thin took the basket. Ladipo quickly turned himself into a coconut, sat in the basket, and was carried along with the others.

As they walked the travellers discussed their new servant.

Ladipo and His Masters. *Page 14.*

"We must be careful not to let him see the treasure if he has such sharp eyes," said Thin.

"Oh," said Beard, "we will manage to lose him before we reach the place, and so he will know nothing about it."

"Let us rest here," said Fat, panting and puffing. "I am worn out and very hungry. What is the good of carrying provisions if we eat nothing?"

They sat down under a tree, and Thin said:

"We will eat a coconut—the largest we have."

Now as Ladipo was the largest coconut, he quickly changed into his proper form and stood before them, smiling.

"I did not hear your footsteps, boy!" cried Fat.

"No," said the servant. "I am as silent as a snake."

"And did you find what you had dropped?"

"Yes, an orange, but I was so hungry that I ate it," he replied at once; and after scolding him for eating an orange without permission, they divided a coconut and set off again.

Once again Ladipo found that the basket was very heavy, and he began to wish he had not to carry it. He could not think of a plan to get rid of his load, until the travellers began to complain of thirst.

"I will run forward to discover a well or a pool," suggested the servant eagerly.

"How can you find a pool in the dark?" objected Fat.

"Oh," said the servant, "I have the ears of an antelope and the instinct of a jackal. I will find some water."

But though the travellers thought he had run on ahead, he had really changed himself into a leaf, and lay on top of the provisions in the basket. He felt quite pleased with the trick he had played his masters, but soon found that they were talking about him as they went on.

"This is a foolish servant," grumbled Fat, who was already tired of the weight on his head.

"Foolish? I am more inclined to think he is dangerous," replied Beard. "He has the eyes of a leopard, the silence of a snake, the ears of an antelope, and the instinct of a jackal! I am afraid he may discover the reason for our journey and steal our treasure from us."

"I think he is a very good servant," said Thin, because, of course, it was he who had engaged the boy. "However, if you are afraid of him, the only thing to do is to lose him—but he is sure to follow us!"

They all sighed, and Beard said:

"Well, if I remember the road rightly, there is a deserted hut not far from here where we can sleep for the remainder of the night. We will wake up very early and creep out of the hut while the boy is still asleep, and so leave him behind." He chuckled. "Even with his wonderful instinct it will take him some time to find us, and meanwhile we will dig up the treasure from the foot of the great breadfruit tree, eat all the provisions in the basket and fill it with the gold and ivory. Then if our servant finds us, he must carry the basket again, and he will never guess what wealth it contains!"

They all agreed with this plan, and laughed heartily, and even Ladipo in the basket was pleased with himself, as he now knew all the plans of the travellers. He lay thinking out his own plans too.

He had no desire to dig under the breadfruit tree, and so he decided to leave this hard work for his masters, while he himself . . .

But at this moment Fat, panting and groaning, laid down the basket.

"Oh dear!" he cried. "This is very hot work! I must take a leaf from the basket to fan myself with!"

At this Ladipo at once changed into his natural shape and appeared before them.

"Boy, you are very sudden!" cried Thin.

"Yes, master, I am as sudden as a thunderstorm," replied Ladipo, picking up the basket.

"And did you find water?"

"I found the pool where the elephants come to bathe, but it is muddy and unfit for drinking," was the reply.

"You miserable servant!" cried Beard, and they all fell upon the poor boy and beat him unmercifully.

After this treatment Ladipo was not sorry that he was going to steal the treasure, because he felt that his masters were wicked and did not deserve to possess such wealth.

Shortly after, they reached a hut by the side of the path. The hut was empty, and they all went in to sleep. But Ladipo stayed awake until he heard his three masters snoring, when he softly changed himself into a grass mat and lay down on the floor, sleeping peacefully.

At dawn Beard awoke and roused his two companions. They could not find their servant, and thought that he must have gone into the forest searching for water.

"All the better!" said Fat. "Now we have really lost him."

They hastily rolled up the mat which lay on the ground and put it on top of the basket. Then they set off as fast as they could go.

Thin carried the basket, but they had not gone far when he began to grumble about the weight.

"It will be much heavier than this when it is full of gold!" declared Beard.

"In that case, why don't you carry it now while it is light?" retorted Thin; and so Beard had to carry the basket.

After a while he, too, began to feel weary, and passed the basket on to Fat. But Fat was the laziest of the three, and filled the air with complaints about the cruelty of his comrades in making him carry their load. At last he laid down the basket.

"It is impossible to carry this monstrous load!" he said. "I shall throw away this stupid grass mat, which we really do not need."

So he threw away the mat, and they went on.

Ladipo had no desire to remain behind, so he flew into the basket in the form of a mosquito, and then changed himself into a pineapple, in case they should try to drive the insect away.

Soon afterwards Fat again decided to throw away the heaviest things in the basket—the coconuts and pineapples.

"What a lazy man he is!" grumbled Ladipo, when he found himself on the ground again with the rest of the fruit. He changed himself into a bird and flew after them, but found that they had all stopped at the foot of a great tree.

"Here we are!" said Thin.

"At last!" said Beard.

"I am nearly dead with fatigue!" said Fat.

The little bird perched on the tree and watched them. How

hard they worked! Even Fat had to help with the digging, and the treasure seemed to be buried in a very deep hole indeed, because it took them quite a long time to find it.

In the end they were successful, and, squatting on the ground, made haste to eat up all the contents of the basket, which they filled with the treasure.

They were all eager to carry the basket now, though it was much heavier than before, and they cast doubtful looks at one another, as if each suspected the other two of plotting to run away with the whole treasure.

They had not gone very far when, with a fierce trumpeting noise, a huge elephant crashed its way through the trees and came in their direction. They were so terrified that they dropped the basket and ran away as fast as their legs would carry them.

The elephant, however, did not pursue them, but took up the basket with its trunk and followed the forest-path almost to within sight of the town. Then the animal disappeared and Ladipo stood there, holding the basket.

He went boldly into the town, and sold the treasure for a great deal of money, with which he bought a large house and a coconut plantation.

He never saw his masters Thin, Fat, and Beard again, and lived happily to the end of his days.

V. Tortoise and Crab

Now both Tortoise and Crab carry a shell-house on their backs, but while Crab can defend himself with his vigorous claws, Tortoise has to rely upon wit for his protection.

Buried in the warm sand of the beach one morning, Crab awoke to hear Tortoise near by calling out: "Gidigbo! Gidigbo! Gidigbo!" which is the call to wrestling.

"Ho!" said Crab, crawling out of his sandy bed. "Who is this who boasts his strength so loudly to the world?"

"Gidigbo! Gidigbo! Gidigbo! I am a mighty warrior! Who will wrestle with me?" repeated Tortoise, wagging his head arrogantly.

"What! Tortoise? You weak little creature," said Crab, with scorn, "how dare you presume to invite me to fight with you?"

"We are both warriors," said Tortoise. "We are clad in armour, but you know very well that I am both braver and stronger than you."

"We shall see!" replied Crab grimly, and he suddenly seized Tortoise by the neck with his sharp pincers. "Now, Tortoise, admit that you are nothing but a foolish boaster," he said triumphantly.

Poor Tortoise closed his eyes and felt quite faint with the pressure on his neck. It was, in fact, impossible for him to reply, and, seeing this, Crab released his hold for a moment, and Tortoise promptly drew his head and feet safely inside his shell.

"Oh, Crab!" he murmured, somewhat faintly, it is true, "now pinch me if you can!"

The Crab, of course, could not find any spot where his claws

20

could take hold of Tortoise, and in the end had to give up the attempt.

"Now," said Tortoise, still keeping his head well out of reach, "I think we ought to agree that we are both equally powerful, and that our armour makes us absolutely secure from attack, once we are on our guard."

"Why, yes!" agreed Crab. "And so we are the strongest and most powerful creatures in the world. Nothing can harm us."

At that moment two boys were passing.

"Ha!" said the one. "Here is a nice big crab—my mother will enjoy it for her evening meal."

And picking up Crab from behind, he popped him into his bag.

"Why, here is a large tortoise," cried his companion. "I shall boil him down and sell his shell in the market-place. How lucky we are to-day!"

He picked up Tortoise without ceremony and took him away.

Since that day the descendants of Tortoise and Crab have always shunned one another, and should Tortoise see the powerful claws of Crab approaching, he pops his head into his shell, and no doubt blushes with shame to think how the two boasters once came to such a sad and undignified end in the cooking-pot.

VI. The Golden Comb

As far as one can see, all along the border of the ocean stretches the shining golden sand. In the daytime the shore is deserted, but at night, when the moon sheds a clear radiance, the water-mammies, or mermaids, rise up out of the sea and sit upon the sand on their silvery tails, combing their long hair, and singing tunes that are like the sighing of the wind in very tall palm trees.

Each mermaid has one great treasure, which she guards closely—her golden comb.

At dawn the moon fades and the mermaids glide into the sea once more, and dance in the green foam or dive to the very bottom of the ocean, where the pearls and corals are, and where fishes swim slowly past with staring eyes.

Once upon a time a careless mermaid slipped back into the sea at dawn and left her comb lying upon the sands.

Oh, how vast and silent were the golden sands that morning! There was not a single footprint anywhere, until a certain fisherman came slowly along, singing to himself, for he had made a good catch of fish that night. In the sunlight he suddenly found the golden comb gleaming. He picked it up, and when he saw how beautiful it was, he ran to his hut and called his family together.

"Ayo," said the fisherman joyfully to his wife, "see what a pretty thing I found upon the sands after I had brought in my nets. Our little daughter Remi shall wear this yellow comb in her hair."

A Fisherman Finds the Golden Comb. *Page 22.*

"Oh," cried little Remi, dancing with delight, "it will be the envy of all the other girls. Let me wear it at once!"

But Taiwo and Kehinde, the twin sons of the fisherman, looked closely at the comb and whispered together.

"Father," they both said at once, "this comb is too pretty for a fisherman's daughter. Let us sell it in the town, for it seems to be made of gold, and with the money we obtain we can buy Remi a comb of tortoiseshell, and other things for ourselves besides."

At this Remi began to cry and begged for the yellow comb. Her brothers just as eagerly wished to sell it, so that in the end their father was quite distracted, and, unwilling to grieve any of them, he decided to take the comb into the town and find out its real value.

Accordingly he set out, after hastily drinking a bowl of gari, which is what poor people live on in Nigeria, and soon reached the town.

He found himself in the market and showed his comb to a trader of good reputation, who examined it—at first carelessly, then with great interest.

"My friend," said the honest trader, who was called Oniyun. "You must take this comb to the goldsmith, not to a poor stall-holder like myself, for if I turned all my goods into money I could still not afford to buy it from you. How came you by such a treasure?"

The cautious fisherman declined to say, and, while thanking Oniyun for his kindness, asked for the name of a goldsmith to whom he might apply.

"You will find an honest man living at the second house in the street leading to the market-place," said the trader. "His name is Alagbede, and he will give you a good price for your comb, which is made of the purest gold and displays the finest work-manship in the world in its decoration. I pray you at least to hide the comb carefully, and to avoid those who wear their garments tucked up.° And should this comb bring you a fortune, I shall expect to be a guest at your feast!"

°Thieves, because they are dressed ready for running.

The fisherman again thanked him and set out for the goldsmith's house. The servants of the rich smith did not at first wish to admit one so poorly clad, but he was persistent in demanding to see their master, and at length they ushered him into a darkened room, where the goldsmith was lying on a divan, enjoying the coolness of a fan. The heat of the day was intense, and he was evidently angry at being disturbed.

"Sir," said the fisherman humbly, "I have here a comb which I desire to sell. I was directed to you by a trader named Oniyun."

On beholding the comb the goldsmith at once lost his air of indolence, and examined it with close attention.

"How came you by this comb?" he demanded, frowning suspiciously.

"Sir," replied the fisherman with dignity, thrusting the comb into his garments, "I obtained the comb by no dishonest means, and if you hold me in suspicion, I have nothing to say to you but 'Eku iyonu!'—Greetings to you on your inquisitiveness!—and to take my departure."

But the goldsmith begged him not to be offended, and made him sit down on a handsomely carved stool.

"Pardon my rashness," he said, "but in our trade we have to be suspicious. The comb you have shown me is of great value, and worthy to adorn the head of the King's favourite wife."

The fisherman was so delighted that he desired to dance for joy, and only kept to his seat with difficulty.

"Oniyun did well to direct your innocent steps to my dwelling," pursued the goldsmith. "Many a one would offer you a bag of cowries for the comb, while concealing its true value from you; and then, after your departure, sell it to a wealthy chief for a large fortune."

"It is true," agreed the fisherman, but somewhat impatiently, as he was so eager to learn the value of the comb.

Finally, after much consideration, the goldsmith named a sum which caused the poor fisherman to go into a transport.

"Sir!" he exclaimed, seizing the goldsmith's feet, "you are indeed an elephant of justice! There are certainly many honest men in the world. May your generosity be rewarded!"

All this time the fisherman's family had been awaiting his

return in great impatience. What was their surprise to see him arrive followed by a cart, drawn by two men, containing many bags of money.

They overwhelmed him with questions and soon heard all the good news.

"I must run to the market-place, and buy silk and velvet clothes to wear!" cried Ayo, his wife.

"Not so fast!" said the fisherman with dignity. "Your days of running to and fro are ended, wife, and you shall not leave the hut until I have procured a ricksha and coolies, so that you may ride about the town like a great lady. The treasure which I found upon the sands has raised us from poverty to wealth, and we are now not poor fisherfolk, but people of importance. To-night we must give a feast which will ever be remembered by the owners of canoes and fishing-nets. Let us therefore prepare."

Within an hour six hired cooks were busy over the huge iron cooking-pots, and sellers of provisions in the market had received orders which made them open their eyes wide with astonishment, and wonder what fish this poor man had caught in his net, that he who had previously consumed only fish and gari should to-day make preparations for such a banquet.

A whole ox, three sheep, and forty chickens were roasted or stewed at the fisherman's hut, so that the savoury odour was carried far and wide. There were bowls of rice and yams, and the most delicious fruit in great abundance, while the best drummers of the town were engaged to play for the dancing.

By the light of the moon the great feast took place, and the poor fishermen left their nets idle and their canoes drawn up on the beach. Never before or since was there such a memorable feast on that sea-shore.

Meanwhile the mermaids were busy preparing to come up to the beach for their midnight revels.

"Are you all ready, daughters?" asked the King of the Water-People. "Have you all got your coral beads and your pearls and your golden combs?"

"Alas!" sobbed the Careless Mermaid, "I have lost my comb."

"What! Your beautiful golden comb?"

"I have looked everywhere—in the caves, and among the seaweeds, but I could not find it. I have asked the shark and the swordfish if they have swallowed it, and they knew nothing about it. I asked the crab if he has tried to hide it in the gravel, but he was quite rude to me. And when I asked the octopus, he tried to grasp me with his horrible, twining arms, so I swam away."

The King of the Water-People looked very grave, and the mermaids all frowned upon their careless sister.

"I have reigned here for thousands and thousands of years," declared the King, shaking his head solemnly, "and not one comb has been lost during all that time. It is true that Land-People have dived into the sea and stolen some of our pearls, and it is true that now and again a broken coral necklace has been washed up on the shore, but a golden comb has never yet become the property of a Land-Maiden. Alas! alas! Oh, careless daughter, you must have left your comb upon the sands."

Anxiously the mermaids crept up the sands in the moonlight and searched vainly for their missing treasure. No trace of it could be found. The Careless Mermaid wept bitterly, and the rest scolded and slapped her. In the distance they could hear music and dancing; the feast of the fisherfolk was at its height.

At dawn the mermaids had to glide back into their watery kingdom, and ever since then all day long they lash their tails and whip the waves into foam and froth, because they are wild with anger that the golden comb should have been taken from them. That is why the surf beats so fiercely all along the coast.

But some day another careless water-mammy may leave her comb behind at dawn, and if you go to the sands early enough and quietly enough, before there is a single footprint, you too may find it gleaming there and make a great fortune, while the surf rages furiously and a little mermaid weeps sadly under the waves for her lost treasure.

VII. The Farmer's Daughter

There once was a farmer who had a very foolish daughter called Molara. She was so foolish that her brothers and sisters often made fun of her and teased her about her stupidity, until poor Molara would hide in a corner of the house and weep bitterly.

Now her father, the farmer, was a rich man, and he had a great many cattle and goats, fields of maize and many fruit trees.

Not far away lived a young farmer who had met with bad fortune. His crops were ruined and his cattle had fallen ill and died, so that he was very poor indeed.

One day he was standing by the wall which divided his land from the fields of his rich neighbour, when he saw the farmer's daughter walking in the field, weeping sadly.

He called to her: "Why do you weep?"

And she replied: "Because I am so ugly."

"If you will give me some good fat cows," said the cunning young man, "I will tell you how to become beautiful."

"But I have no cows," Molara replied sadly.

"What are those animals I can see in the field?"

"Those are my father's cows."

"Well, if you will bring me half your father's cows, I will tell you the secret."

Foolish Molara joyfully drove half the herd of cows into the young man's field.

"The secret is this," said the young man. "To be beautiful you must smile all the time."

Molara ran smiling into the house, and her brothers and sisters exclaimed:

"Just look at Molara! She is quite pretty tonight!"

But when the farmer came home, he was in great distress, because half his cattle had disappeared and could not be found anywhere.

Molara said nothing.

The next day the young man stood at the wall again, and saw the farmer's daughter walking in the field.

"Are you happy now?" he called to her.

"No," she replied sadly, "I am still unhappy, because no one will marry me."

"Well," said the crafty young man, "if you will bring me the rest of your father's cattle, I will tell you how to get married."

So foolish Molara gaily drove the rest of the cattle into his field, and he said:

"The secret is this: pretend that you do not wish to marry anyone, and all the young men will be anxious to marry you."

Molara ran into the house and found her eldest brother sitting with his friends.

"Poor Molara!" said the brother. "She looks so pretty now, but no one will marry her."

"I shall never marry!" declared Molara, smiling brightly, and her brother's friends were so much astonished that they all resolved to ask her father if one of them might marry her.

But when the farmer came home, he would not listen to them. He was very angry and distressed because the rest of his cattle had disappeared and could not be found anywhere.

And Molara said nothing.

Next day the young man stood by the wall and called to her as she walked in the field:

"Are you happy now?"

"No," said Molara sadly, "I am still unhappy, because everyone says I am so foolish."

"Well," said the wicked young man, "if you will bring me your father's goats, I will tell you the secret of wisdom."

Molara gladly drove her father's goats into the young man's field, and he said:

"This is the secret of wisdom: remember that everybody else is more foolish than yourself."

Molara ran back into the house. She smiled, and turned her back on all the young men, and when anyone spoke to her, she had a wise look, as if to say: "Ah! You think I am foolish, but I know you are much more foolish than I!"

So that everybody looked at her with pleasure and respect, and she was at last very happy.

But when the farmer came home, he wept and said:

"Alas, children! I am ruined. My cattle and goats have disappeared by magic, and I am sure that in the morning the harvest will be gone from my fields and the fruit from my trees. Alas! alas!"

And still Molara said nothing.

But she lay awake all night thinking of her father's words, and as she was now much less foolish, she realized how wicked the young man was, in spite of his good advice, and she tried to think of some plan by which she could get back her father's cattle and goats.

Very early next morning she went to the market, and saw the young man's wife buying rice for the day. Molara went up to her and said:

"If you will give me the goats which are in your husband's field, I will tell you a great secret about him."

The wife was at once filled with curiosity to know the secret about her husband, and finally she agreed to drive back the goats. When Molara had counted them and seen that they were all safe in her father's field, she said:

"This is the secret: your husband is a dishonest man."

The wife was very angry to hear this, and wished she had not handed over the goats, but it was too late. That evening Molara's father returned home rejoicing.

"Wonderful! My goats have returned! . . . Molara, how pretty you look!"

And Molara went to bed smiling.

Early next morning she went again to the market and saw the young mans' wife.

"If you give me half of the cattle in your husband's field," she said, "I will tell you an even greater secret about him."

The wife was very eager to know the secret, and could not

help driving half the cattle into Molara's field. When she had counted them, Molara said:

"This is the secret: your husband will always be poor while he is dishonest."

The wife went away in a fury, wishing she had not given up the cattle.

That night the farmer came home in high spirits.

"Still more wonderful!" he declared. "Half my cattle have returned. I am a very lucky man! . . . Molara, these three young men have asked me if they can marry you, and I cannot decide which of them will be the best husband."

Molara turned her back on them all and went to bed smiling.

The next morning she saw the young man's wife and said:

"If you will give me the rest of the cattle in your husband's field, I will tell you the most important secret of all about him."

"I do not wish to know your secrets!" said the wife rudely. "And besides, my husband will beat me when he comes home and finds his field empty."

"Very well, then," said Molara, and pretended to go away. But the wife was really devoured with anxiety to know the secret, and she ran after Molara and promised to drive back all the remaining cattle.

When Molara had counted them all, she said:

"This is the secret, and I hope you will repeat my words to your husband, if he asks you what has happened to the cattle and goats. Your husband thinks he is wise, but he is much more foolish than I!"

That night there was great rejoicing and feasting in the rich farmer's house.

"All my cattle and goats have returned by magic!" cried the farmer, embracing his children. "I am a lucky man. . . . Molara, you look so wise and pretty; I shall not accept any man as a son-in-law unless he has at least twenty cows and ten servants, because really I have a very good daughter."

Molara smiled as she went to bed. But no one ever knew just how foolish and just how wise she had been!

VIII. The Seven Brothers

Once there lived a man—a very old man—who had seven handsome sons, a large house and many tall trees around it. One morning he said to his eldest son:

"Adekunle, I would like you to climb that tree opposite the house and bring me down some fruit."

"With pleasure, father," replied the boy, and going out of the house he began to climb the tree.

But when he had climbed only half way up, he suddenly gave a cry and fell down to the ground, and when the second son ran to him, he found that he was dead.

"Alas, father!" cried the second son. "Adekunle is dead! I will climb up and get the fruit."

But when the second son was only half way up the tree, he too gave a cry and fell to the ground, and when the third brother ran to him he was dead.

"Alas, father!" cried the third son. "My two brothers are dead. I will get you the fruit."

But the same thing happened to him and to all the brothers in turn, even to the youngest. There they lay in a row on the ground, and their father and mother wept to see what had befallen.

"This is terrible!" said the father. "I will climb up myself to get the fruit."

But his wife begged him not to climb the tree.

"There is some mystery in this," she said. "Let us go to the King and tell him what has happened."

The old man agreed, and they went together to the King's

32

palace. The King declared that it was the strangest thing he had ever heard of, and that he would give a quarter of his kingdom to anyone who could solve the mystery of the seven brothers, and why they fell dead when they reached the same place in climbing the tree.

All the magicians of the country resolved to find out the reason, and they set off in great haste from every direction to the old man's house.

There stood the tree, and there lay the seven brothers, just as he had said. The magicians were all eager to climb the tree, but one who was considered more powerful than the rest was at length allowed to climb the tree.

When he was half way up, he too gave a cry and fell to the ground dead.

At this the other magicians were filled with horror and ran away from the place—all except one, a very wise man, who waited until all the others had gone far away, and then went by himself to look at the seven brothers and the first magician, who lay in a row on the ground at the foot of the tree.

But he was much too cautious to climb the tree.

Instead, he brought an axe and chopped the tree down. It fell with a crash, and after looking at it carefully, and putting something in a basket which he carried, the magician hurried away, laughing gleefully.

Now at this very moment who should pass by but Tortoise, on his way home to supper.

Like all inquisitive people, Tortoise went about with his ears and eyes ready for news. He had heard about the mystery of the seven brothers, and when he saw the Very Wise Magician go away chuckling to himself so happily, he said;

"Now I am sure that this magician has solved the mystery, and that he feels sure of winning a quarter of the kingdom. I must learn more about this!"

And so, instead of going home to supper, he followed the magician very quietly to his house and hid in a dark corner.

While the magician's wife was preparing supper, her husband was very busy in a dark part of the house, mixing herbs and charms in a little jar. Then while he was enjoying the savoury stew which she had prepared, he began to tell her all about the seven brothers, and Tortoise crawled a little nearer and listened very hard.

"Of course," said the magician, "it would have been very foolish to climb the tree, so I chopped it down instead; and what do you think I found?"

His wife did not know, so he continued proudly:

"Well, curled up round a branch just at the very spot where the seven brothers and the first magician paused and fell to the ground, was a monstrous snake. As each brother reached the branch, the snake bit him and he fell to the ground. But when I chopped down the tree, the snake was crushed by the fall. . . . I have him in my basket."

The wife cried out with admiration, and even Tortoise could not help being struck by the sagacity of the Very Wise Magician.

"And now I will tell you a funny thing," added the magician. "These seven brothers and the first magician are not dead at all! They are merely in a trance caused by the bite of that poisonous snake! I have only to pour into their mouths a little of the charm contained in this small jar, and they will once more be restored to life."

The wife, of course, was delighted, and she and her husband began to plan what they would do with the reward promised by the King.

Tortoise, however, lay low, and remained very quiet until they were fast asleep, when he crept out and hunted for the jar containing the charm. At last he found it, and poured the liquid into another jar. Then he filled the first jar with water and put it back exactly where he had found it.

Very early in the morning Tortoise went to a hunter in the forest and asked him for a dead snake.

"A dead snake!" cried the hunter in astonishment.

"Yes," said Tortoise, "but I am in a great hurry. I pray you, if you have a snake, put it in this basket at once."

"I only killed one snake yesterday," replied the hunter doubtfully, "and its head is very badly crushed, so perhaps it is of no use to you?"

"It will do very well!" replied Tortoise eagerly. "I will not forget your kindness when I am rich."

Then, with his basket and the jar containing the charm, he set off for the King's palace. When he was admitted to the King's presence he said very humbly:

"Sire, I have had the good fortune to solve the mystery of the seven brothers."

The whole Court was greatly astonished.

"What! Tortoise!" exclaimed the King. "I never thought you were so clever, but if you can explain the mystery, I will keep to my promise and give you a quarter of the kingdom."

Just then the magician arrived, smiling happily, and quite confident that no one else could have discovered the solution.

"Sire," he said, bowing low before the King. "I have solved the mystery of the seven brothers."

"You are too late," said the King. "Someone else has made the discovery before you."

The magician looked round and saw only Tortoise.

"Tortoise!" he exclaimed, laughing. "Why, I have often kicked Tortoise out of my way. He is making fun of you all. He cannot possibly have solved the mystery."

"But, indeed, I have, and I am only waiting to tell my story."

The King commanded Tortoise to explain the mystery, and with much enjoyment he began:

"Well, Your Majesty, to begin with, I was far too cautious to climb the tree, and instead I took an axe and chopped the tree down, and in the branches I found . . . a huge snake, which must have bitten each of the brothers, so that they cried out and fell to the ground. And here in my basket is the snake, whose head was crushed when the tree was chopped down!"

A murmur of applause went through the Court, and the King, turning to the Very Wise Magician, asked:

"And what is your explanation?"

"Sire," replied the bewildered magician, "my story is exactly the same, but I assure you that I, and I alone, discovered the secret, that I chopped down the tree, and that the snake in my basket is the real one, and the only one which bit the seven brothers!"

The King looked at Tortoise and the magician and at the two snakes, and could not decide which was the true claim. Then a happy thought struck the magician.

"One moment, Sire!" he cried. "I have another proof. I have discovered that the seven brothers and the first magician are not really dead at all, but only in a trance, and I have in this little jar a wonderful charm which will restore them to life."

The King looked enquiringly at Tortoise, who replied:

"It is true that the seven brothers are not dead, and I have in this small jar the only charm in the world which will restore them to life."

"This can soon be decided," said the King, and he sent a number of slaves to the house of the old man to bring back the bodies of the seven brothers and the first magician.

The King then commanded the Very Wise Magician to restore them all to life. The magician poured a little of the liquid from his jar into the mouth of each and sat down, smiling calmly, to watch the result.

But nothing happened! After a while the magician began to tremble with fear and disappointment.

Then Tortoise took up his own jar and poured the charm into the mouths of the brothers and the first magician. Instantly they all sat up and began to ask one another questions.

The delighted parents rushed to greet their children, newly restored to life, and they were so excited that they embraced Tortoise too, and thanked him with tears in their eyes. The first magician also was joyfully welcomed by his friends.

"Tortoise," said the King, "you have done a very good and a very clever deed. A quarter of my kingdom is yours."

The rascal Tortoise accepted the reward and then turned to the unfortunate magician, who lay on the ground in a state of collapse.

"Unfortunate man!" he said. "You have often made fun of Tortoise and kicked him cruelly out of your path. This is your reward, for his wit is keener than yours, in spite of all your magic arts. May this be a lesson to you! And to show you how generous I am, I will give you a large house to live in, and a prosperous farm to work on, so that you may be kept out of mischief and have nothing more to do with false charms."

But the poor magician was so greatly astounded by the words of Tortoise and by all that had happened, that he could make no reply, and he spent the rest of his life in silence, wondering how Tortoise had managed to outwit him.

IX. The Bat

The Bat has wings like a bird, but a body like his cousin the Rat. He is very sly and timid, and all the other creatures detest him, but in particular for the following reason.

Once the rats were at war with the birds. The battle was very fierce. Now and then a bird would swoop down and pounce on a rat, and then the rats did their best to seize their enemy by the wings or tail-feathers and tear him to pieces.

The rats were very hard pressed, and at last they sent an urgent message to their cousin, Bat, asking him to come and help them in the fight. Bat agreed to join them, and he fought on their side for some time, until he found that the birds were likely to be victorious.

As soon as he saw this, he deserted his friends and flew up into the air to join the birds. In the end the birds won the battle and the rats had to run back to their holes and hide.

Bat was very much excited and expected the birds to reward him handsomely for his assistance, but instead they drove him away in disgust, crying:

"We have no use for a traitor!"

Bat fluttered down to the ground, feeling very sore from the pecking he had just received. But the rats would not make friends with him after his desertion, and they too drove him angrily away.

Poor Bat was now sorry for the way in which he had acted, but it was too late, and ever since then he has been shunned by all creatures, and forced to hide all day in some dark place and to come out only at night, when his enemies cannot see him and call after him:

"We have no use for a traitor!"

X. The Two Jars

O nce upon a time there lived a mighty hunter named Ogun-funminire. In addition to this long name he had several sons, all hunters like himself, so that eventually his family came to be known throughout the land for their skill and courage in tracking the wild beasts of the forest.

Ogunfunminire lived to be a very, very old man, so that he saw his children's children's children around him, or, in other words, he was a great-grandfather.

But having reached such a vast age, Ogunfunminire, alas! began to grow too feeble to be successful in the hunt, and to his great sorrow, his sons, grandsons, and great-grandsons would slip off very early in the morning into the forest so that they need not take the old man with them.

"Alas! alas!" cried Ogunfunminire to himself. "I am no longer the mighty hunter whose exploits were related throughout the land. I am nothing but a feeble old man, and my children have no patience with me. Yet hunt I must, for I shall die of grief if I must stay at home like other old men."

He therefore made a long journey through the forest until he reached the hut of a magician who lived all alone in the middle of a marsh, with snakes and lizards and crocodiles for his only neighbours.

"O great magician of the marsh!" said Ogunfunminire, trembling as he drew near the hut. "Tell me, I pray you, how I may continue to hunt in the forest, as I did long ago in the days of my youth."

For some time the magician said nothing at all, but at last he spoke:

"Why do you not stay at home with the other old men, Ogunfunminire?"

"Because," replied Ogunfunminire boldly, "I wish to be a hunter to the end of my days, and if you will help me, I will give you this golden chain, which is of great value."

For a long time again the magician said nothing, but in the end he took the chain, and disappeared inside his hut. When he returned, he carried two jars, which he gave to Ogunfunminire, saying:

"When you desire to hunt, dip your head into the first jar, with these words: 'Jar! Jar! If there is any virtue in you, change me!' And when you are weary of hunting, you must dip your head into the second jar, and all will be well."

Ogunfunminire was greatly puzzled by the words of the magician, but he thanked him, and carried the two jars home and hid them secretly in a private room of his house.

Early the next morning he went into the room and dipped his head into the first jar, saying in a trembling voice: "Jar! Jar! If there is any virtue in you, change me!"

To his astonishment, he was at once changed into a serpent, and in this form he glided out into the forest and hunted to his heart's content all the day long. When evening came, he returned to his house, and dipped his head into the second jar, when he at once regained his proper form.

Now Ogunfunminire's hunting days began all over again, and nobody could think why he seemed so happy, and where he spent all his time, for during the day he was nowhere to be found.

But one day his eldest son came into the room where the two jars were hidden, just at the moment when the old man was uttering the magic words.

When he saw how his father was changed into a serpent, the son, who was himself an old man, was filled with horror, and hastened to tell the whole family about the jars and the secret of Ogunfunminire's happiness.

Now the old hunter knew no peace, for his children and grandchildren and great-grandchildren spent the whole time in trying to persuade him to remain at home instead of wandering in the forest in such a terrible form. But he would not listen to them, and every day dipped his head into the first jar and glided out of the house in the shape of a serpent.

At last one day the family was celebrating the birth of Ogunfunminire's first great-great-grandchild, but the old man could not be found to join in the festivities. He was away in the forest, and in a sudden passion one of his sons kicked at the two jars, so that they were both overturned, and the charm was spilt on the ground.

At night Ogunfunminire returned and glided into the room to dip his head in the second jar. But alas! the jar was empty. In a frenzy the hunter in his serpent's form tried to find a few drops of the precious charm, but it had all soaked deep into the earth and was lost for ever.

Now, indeed, the unfortunate old man wished that he had taken his children's advice, and remained quietly at home.

Poor Ogunfunminire! How he envied the other old men who sat at the door of their houses in the cool of the evening relating old adventures instead of trying to find new ones in the forest.

For three days the serpent glided sadly round and round the house, while his family shut all the doors and were afraid to venture out.

At the end of the third day the serpent returned to the depths of the forest and was never seen again, but from that time—and even now in Nigeria—the descendants of Ogunfunminire bear the title "Orile," which means "Son-of-a-mighty-serpent."

XI. Akiti

Once there was a famous hunter and wrestler named Akiti, who was victorious in every wrestling-match in which he took part.

But his success was due not entirely to his own strength and quickness, but to a wonderful charm which he wore, in the form of a ring. Every time Akiti called to his ring, his wish was fulfilled, and as he had always wished for success in wrestling, no one had yet been found who could overthrow him.

At last Akiti came to be considered the strongest man in the land, and he declared himself king of the forest as well.

"Ho! ho!" laughed the wolf, when he heard this. "I will soon show him who is king of the forest!"

But when they met to fight, Akiti spoke to his ring and quickly overthrew the wolf, and after this he was prouder than ever.

"What is this?" cried the leopard. "Akiti says he is king of the forest! I will show him how mistaken he is."

But the leopard, too, was overthrown, and Akiti sang:
"I am king of the forest! I am king of the forest!"

"Ho! ho!" growled the lion. "A weak human says he is king of the forest! That shall never be!"

And he came to fight with Akiti, but the hunter sprang on him and broke his back with one twist of his mighty arms. Now Akiti felt quite sure that he was king of the forest, and did not expect anyone else to oppose his claim.

One day he was out hunting when he met the elephant.

"I am king of the forest!" cried Akiti.

"No! I am king of the forest!" trumpeted the elephant

Akiti Fights the Elephant. *Page 44.*

defiantly, and they began to fight. Both were very strong, and the elephant was more cunning than most animals and knew many charms.

Finding that he could not win by strength, Akiti suddenly changed himself into a snake, and, creeping on the ground, tried to bite the elephant. But the elephant's hide was tough, and with his huge feet he tried to stamp on the snake, so Akiti quickly changed himself into a poisoned arrow, and tried to pierce the elephant's head.

But the elephant seized the arrow in his trunk and was just about to break it in two, when Akiti changed himself into a mosquito and flew into his enemy's big, flapping ear.

He found his way down right inside the elephant's body, and hunted about until he came to his enemy's heart.

Then he changed himself back into his own shape and began to cut at the heart, while the elephant rushed about, stamping and trumpeting. At last Akiti had cut the heart right in two, and the elephant fell dead. Akiti cut his way out with his hunter's knife and stood on the elephant's body, shouting:

"I am Akiti, the mighty hunter, king of the forest!"

And this time there was no one to contradict him!

XII. The Elegant Crab

Mother and Father Crab were very proud of their daughter. To begin with, her back was so smooth and her claws were so delicate!

They sent her away to another country to be educated in the most elegant manner and to learn all the accomplishments possible to a young lady crab.

After a long absence the daughter returned home, and her parents gave a party in her honour, inviting their friends and relations—even the most distant ones—their cousin the lobster, their neighbours the jellyfish and limpets, and the charming family of prawns and shrimps.

When all the guests were assembled, the young lady Crab was called in by her mother to show off the accomplishments she had learnt while abroad.

She advanced coyly towards the company, moving sideways, as crabs always do.

"Good gracious!" cried the guests, looking greatly astonished. "To think that after being so long in another country your daughter still walks sideways! How disgraceful! Has she not learnt to swim gracefully like a fish, or to glide like a snake?"

"Indeed, no!" retorted the Mother Crab. "Whatever accomplishments my daughter learns, I desire her first of all to be a good crab, not an indifferent fish or snake. Of what use to the world, may I ask, is a crab which is ashamed to walk like a crab and prefers to swim or glide like somebody quite different?"

"You are a wise mother," said the old lobster. "It is better to make the most of what we really are, than to adopt the ways of others which do not suit us."

XIII. Tortoise and Fly

Times were hard. Tortoise and his large family barely had enough to eat, and they would remember with regret the good meals they had had in more prosperous times, and wish that they need never feel hungry again.

"Have you noticed," said Nyanribo to her husband, "how prosperous Fly and his family seem to be? Even in these hard times they seem to have plenty of money and buy provisions in the market every day. I am sure there is some mystery in it."

Tortoise thought so too, but when he went round to the house of the Fly family, he found nobody at home. He waited, resting in the shade of a paw-paw tree, and soon Fly returned, carrying a large and heavy sack.

Tortoise was very curious to know what was in the sack, but he was not bold enough to ask, and as Fly made no attempt to open it in his presence, he made his farewell greeting and went away.

But he did not immediately go home. Instead, he crept round to the back of the house and put his eye close to a space in the wall, so that he could see what was going on inside the house.

He saw that Fly was opening his sack, and out of it poured cowries and coins of every sort, so that Tortoise's eyes nearly popped out of his head with wonder and envy.

How came the humble Fly to discover such a treasure? Lucky Fly! He could spread his little wings and buzz through the air without anyone knowing his business or his destination. This is what Tortoise was thinking as he went sadly home.

But the next evening he returned secretly to Fly's house and once more applied his inquisitive eye to the hole in the wall. The house was empty, but Fly soon returned, carrying the same heavy sack, which proved to be full of the same treasure. Fly packed the money away, and laid the sack down in a corner near the door.

When all were sound asleep in the house, Tortoise, carrying a small bag, crept into the room and hid himself in the sack, for he was determined to find out the secret of Fly's wealth.

Early next morning Fly shouldered the sack, not without a sigh, for it seemed heavier than usual; but he was eager to be off, and did not look inside.

He flew through the air for some distance, and then came down in the market-place of a large village, where drummers were beating the tones of a dance.

The village maidens danced, and the rest of the people watched them and threw coins to the drummers when the dancing was good. When one of the maidens danced very well, the drummers were showered with coins and cowries.

Hiding in the grass behind the drummers, Fly would pounce down and steal the coins, unobserved, pulling them one by one into his sack, until a good pile had been collected and it was nearly night-time.

"So this is Fly's treasure!" thought Tortoise, shaking with laughter inside the sack, and he filled his own little bag with coins, and then lay still.

At last Fly took up the sack and flew away home, groaning at the weight of the sack. When he reached the house, he flung down the sack, complaining to his wife that he had never known it to be so heavy. While he was talking, Tortoise crept out of the sack with his bag and stole from the house in the darkness.

What was the disgust of Fly's wife to discover very few coins in the sack—in fact, it was half empty.

While she was scolding Fly for his laziness, Tortoise hurried home with the money, and his family was soon enjoying a feast which lasted late into the night.

Then Tortoise returned and took his place in the sack which lay inside Fly's door, and the next day the same thing happened. The drummers were showered with coins, which Fly collected busily and stored in his sack; and Tortoise chose the best coins and filled his own bag, leaving poor Fly very few indeed.

But this time Fly's suspicions were aroused, and when his wife scolded him for his laziness, he said:

"Be quiet, wife! There is some mystery in this. The sack was very heavy indeed, and now it is light. Our money has been stolen."

Poor Fly was trying to think how the money could have been stolen, when Tortoise softly entered the room where all the family were supposed to be fast asleep, and crawled into the sack. Fly pretended to sleep like the rest, but his sharp eyes had seen the thief, and he was filled with pleasure.

"Now I have him!" he thought, and fell sound asleep.

Next morning Fly was in a very good humour as he prepared to go out. He did not grumble about the weight of the sack, which he tied up securely.

The drummers were playing as usual, and at first Fly stole the coins and placed them in his sack.

After a while he tied up the sack again and began buzzing round one of the drummers until he succeeded in gaining attention.

"Is it true," asked Fly politely, "that for some days you have been losing money, and that you cannot find the thief?"

"It is true, indeed," replied the drummer angrily, "and woe betide the thief when we find him."

"Perhaps I can help you."

The drummer laughed, but Fly pointed to his sack.

"There is the thief. I caught him stealing your coins, and I have tied him up in his own sack."

The drummer took hold of the sack and shook it. Tortoise and the stolen coins rattled loudly.

"Ah!" cried the drummer, "how shall I punish the thief? I will drown him in the river. I will throw him to the crocodiles."

"No," replied Fly; "the crocodiles might refuse to eat such a miserable creature! Why do you not drum him?"

"It is a good idea," said the drummer, chuckling.

He laid the sack in front of him and began to beat upon it with a stick. Tortoise soon cried out for mercy, but the other drummers also came and beat the sack with sticks until the smooth shell of Tortoise was covered with bruises.

At last Fly took up the sack and flew high into the air. When he was above Tortoise's house, he let the sack drop, and it fell with a mighty bang right in front of Tortoise's door.

Out rushed Nyanribo, who found poor Tortoise more dead than alive, and very sorry that he had let his curiosity and envy lead him into such trouble.

To this day he bears upon his back the mark of the bruises he received, but he never told anyone the true story of the beating which he suffered in the sack of his enemy, Fly.

XIV. The Leopard-Man

It was market-day in a certain village on the edge of the forest, and a very handsome stranger walked about the streets, looking at the wares displayed on the stalls, but buying nothing and speaking to nobody.

A girl, who was selling ripe oranges piled in a large calabash, offered him her fruit, but he turned away and said nothing.

Soon afterwards he went into the forest and was not seen again, but the orange-girl, who was named Tunde, remembered him, and could not sleep that night for thinking about the handsome stranger.

Next market-day he came again to the village, and once more Tunde offered him her golden oranges. How sad she was when he turned away and soon after walked back into the gloomy forest!

The third time he came to the village, he again refused to buy Tunde's fruit, but he looked at the girl for a long time, and she fell so much in love with him that when he went back into the forest, she left her oranges on the ground and ran after him.

When he saw her, the stranger stopped and asked:

"Why do you follow me?"

"Because I love you and wish to stay with you in the forest."

"Oh, you must not follow me!" cried the stranger hastily. "Run back to your village and think no more of me."

He walked on, but Tunde ran after him, and he soon stopped and asked her again why she followed him.

"Because I wish to marry you," said poor Tunde.

But the stranger replied:

"Go back and marry a young man from your own village."

He hurried on, and the poor girl followed, weeping bitterly, for a long way, until she was very weary. At last the handsome stranger stood still and looked at her silently.

"My poor girl," he said sadly. "I would gladly marry you, for I love your dark eyes and your bright smile. But if you knew me, you would not wish to follow me at all. I beg you to go back before it is too late. Go back to your village and do not seek to follow me any further."

But Tunde grasped the stranger's hand and said:

"Whoever you are, take pity on me. I cannot leave you. I will follow you, and I am not afraid to stay even here in the dark forest, as your bride."

The stranger sighed heavily and let her walk by his side through the long, dim, green paths of the forest, where strange birds and gorgeous butterflies passed them, and the scent of the sweetest flowers filled all the air.

At last once more the man stopped and said earnestly:

"Will you not leave me quickly, before it is too late?"

"Never!" cried Tunde, weeping, and they went on.

Soon they stopped at the foot of a large tree, and there on the ground lay a leopard skin.

"Alas!" said the stranger. "Do you love me still? I am a leopard, and only once in a week can I go about in the form of a man. Alas! Tunde, your fate is sealed!"

With these words, he stepped into the skin and became a leopard, who crouched down, snarling fiercely and preparing to spring at the girl.

But Tunde was fleet of foot, and was already running down the path as fast as she could go in the direction of the village.

The leopard followed her, crying:

> "Lady, lady, stay with me.
> My companion you must be.
> In the forest you must roam,
> Where the leopard makes his home."

But Tunde paid no heed to the words and ran faster than ever. Sometimes the leopard nearly caught her, but she was so terrified that she went faster than the antelope, and at last the path grew wider, the trees were further apart, and she knew that she was near the edge of the forest.

The leopard kept on singing:

> "Lady, lady, do not flee,
> Stay in these deep woods with me.
> Now escape me if you can,
> You who chose the leopard-man."

Tunde made a last attempt to reach the village. She ran so fast that her feet scarcely touched the ground, and even the leopard could not keep up with her.

How thankful she was when suddenly the huts and the market-place of her own village lay before her! She ran straight into the first hut, without once looking back, and the leopard, who could not follow her so far, crept back snarling into the forest.

Since then the leopard-man has never been seen again in that village, but perhaps the same handsome stranger strolls on market-days in some other village and charms the hearts of village maidens away.

XV. Tortoise and the World's Wisdom

When the world was young, Tortoise was busy for quite a long time collecting wisdom. His task took him a number of years, but at last, looking through all that he had gathered together, he discovered that he had all the world's wisdom there.

At first Tortoise was very happy with this discovery, and he put all the pieces of wisdom into a huge pot, which he hid in a corner of his house. But he was terribly afraid that someone might find out the secret and steal his pot.

He lay awake for three nights wondering where he could hide it in perfect safety.

"Now if I bury it," he thought, "someone may see me dig the hole and look there when I have gone away. And if I sink the pot into the sea, I may never find the place again, and all my work will be wasted."

At last he found the solution.

"I will hide my pot at the top of a tree!" he cried joyfully. "No one will think of looking up there for my treasure, and so it will be perfectly safe until I wish to use it."

"What did you say, my dear?" asked Nyanribo, his wife, waking up.

"Go to sleep, wife! I was only counting how many bunches of bananas we may expect to have on our tree," he replied hastily, for he was so anxious to keep his secret that he had not even told Nyanribo about it.

The next morning he tied a strong cord round his pot and suspended it in front of him. Then he went to the tallest tree in the district and, when no one was about, he began to climb the tree.

But the heavy pot suspended in front of him so impeded his movements that he found it almost impossible to make any progress, and after a while he slipped down to the ground again to rest.

Then he made another attempt, but again without success, and he was still only a short distance from the ground when his son came out of the house and stood watching him.

"Go away," said Tortoise crossly. "Can't you see that I am busy?"

"But, father," cried the son, "you will never get to the top of the tree if you carry the pot in front of you. Why don't you hang it behind you, and then it will be out of your way, and the climbing will be easy?"

Tortoise stopped climbing and thought:

"Well! I have all the world's wisdom in my pot, and yet I am so foolish that my own son can instruct me in climbing a tree. I have put my pieces of wisdom to very poor use!"

He was so disgusted at the thought that he dropped the pot, and it crashed into many pieces, while all the wisdom it had contained was scattered far and wide. And that is why fragments of wisdom are now to be found all over the earth.

XVI. The Iroko Tree

The forest is full of giants, growing in lofty dignity high above the tangled undergrowth, the creepers and the ferns, where snakes and lizards and all the strange wild creatures have their lairs and holes.

But of all the trees, none is as massive and twisted as the iroko. During the day its cool, wide-spreading branches give a pleasing shade from the steaming heat and the burning rays of the sun.

But at night there is a strange light which comes and goes, now hanging on its lower branches, now again right at the top, among the nests of the adventurous birds, or again hovering in the wood near the tree.

And when men see it, they tremble and hurry quickly away, for it is the Iroko-Man, the spirit that dwells in the tree, who comes out at night with his little lamp and flits about the forest.

     ✿   ✿   ✿   ✿   ✿

Wabi the Wanderer sat in a little hut of branches which his servants had made for him in a clearing of the forest.

Wabi was very tired after a long day's journey, and the night was extremely hot. Wabi, who was known among his people as He-whose-feet-have-touched-every-corner-of-the-world, felt discontented and in a very bad temper indeed. He was vexed because night had come too quickly, and he was still some hours' journey away from his home.

"I am a man of great ill-luck!" muttered Wabi to himself, as he lay down on the mat his servants had spread for him in the hut and fell asleep.

Outside the servants were weeping and bewailing their fate,
for their master had just given them a sound beating for being
too slow with their preparations for the night. He was, in fact, a
harsh and cruel master, and during the journey his unfortunate
servants had suffered many hardships because of his unkind-
ness.

Wabi, however, had no thought for them, and, in fact, intend-
ed to give them another beating in the morning, because he was
so angry at having to sleep in the forest when he was only a few
hours from home.

After he had slept a little while, he suddenly awoke, in the
great stillness of the dark forest. He could not help thinking of
ghosts and prowling leopards, and to reassure himself, he
peeped out of the hut.

What was his alarm on discovering that he was absolutely
alone! His servants, smarting from the blows he had given them,
had run away, leaving him to find his way home alone the next
day.

But in a panic Wabi resolved that he could not under any circumstances remain there alone in the middle of the forest. He
wrapped his cloak round his trembling shoulders, took up his
stick, and began to walk through the trees.

The path was rough, and shrubs tripped him up so that he fell
many times. Creepers twined themselves round his feet like
snakes, and altogether he was very terrified, when he suddenly
beheld a little light not far away, between the trees.

Wabi bounded towards the light, thinking he must be near
some village. What was his disgust to find that it was a small
lamp carried by a feeble old man, who blinked at him timidly as
he approached!

"Begone, crocodile!" said Wabi, with his usual rudeness.
"What brings you here at such an hour, with your stupid light?
Curses on you, for you have taken me out of my way."

"I may yet serve you as a guide," replied the old man mildly.
"Why should you greet me with curses and angry looks?"

"I would sooner take a blind monkey as a guide," was the
unfriendly retort.

"Alas!" said the old man, shaking his head. "These are harsh words. But tell me, Wanderer, where have you been? Who are you, and what is your destination? Have you lost your way, or are you in the forest with some company of travellers?"

"Before I met you, old man," said the rough Wabi, "my only intention was to reach home as quickly as possible; but I have on me a sharp knife, and I shall not rest until it has silenced your chattering tongue for ever."

He made as though to draw the knife from his belt, but instantly the old man and his light vanished, and the Wanderer was left, trembling, in complete darkness. But in the branches of an ancient iroko tree, which towered near him, there seemed to be a murmur:

"Wabi the Wanderer, your fate is sealed." And all the trees around sighed: "Sealed! Sealed!"

Wabi laughed scornfully and continued his way, but whichever way he walked, he went always in a circle, and many days later he was found wandering still in the forest, his hair wild, his garments tattered, and on his lips a strange laugh and the words: "Sealed! Sealed! Sealed!"

For Wabi the Wanderer had gone mad.

    ❖   ❖   ❖   ❖   ❖

"Surely," murmured Taiwo the Traveller to himself, "I cannot now be far from home! It is more than a month since I began my journey, and I can still see nothing before me but forest—wild, dense, gloomy forest. How fortunate it is that neither leopard nor wolf, neither snake nor savage ape, has harmed me, though I travel alone and almost defenceless."

Even as he spoke, Taiwo could not help trembling, for night was falling, and as he pressed onwards he could hear around him all the mysterious forest sounds—the whirring of insects, the growl of leopards, the howling of wolves, and the rustling of leaves.

Taiwo wished for a little company, and, in fact, the darkness and loneliness became so oppressive at length that he began singing for the comfort of hearing his own voice.

Suddenly a light flickered some distance in front of him, and again disappeared. Taiwo stood still and listened.

"I am very foolish," he thought. "Here I am singing, forgetting that there may be enemies lurking in the darkness, who may attack me at any moment with spear or poisoned arrows. I must be cautious."

At this instant the light shone again, and gradually came nearer.

Taiwo waited with his knife ready to throw, but when he saw that the light was carried by an old, bent man, walking with a stick, he replaced his knife and hastened to greet the old man.

"Alas! unfortunate one, what have you done to get lost in the middle of the forest at this time of night? Let me guide you to the edge of the forest."

"You yourself seem to be in need of a guide," replied the old man pleasantly. "Where have you been?"

"I am Taiwo the Traveller, and I have been to the city on the great river of the North. I am now on my way home, but I confess that in the darkness the path is hard to find, and I am very solitary. I have at home a little family awaiting me with eagerness, and in this wallet I carry presents for them all from the great city. But I begin to wonder if I shall ever see them! . . ."

"You are courteous and kind," said the old man. "I will guide you."

And with his light he guided Taiwo to the edge of the forest, which was after all not far away. When dawn came the old and the young man stood side by side outside Taiwo's own house.

"Old man," said Taiwo heartily, "you have guided me well. I pray you to enter my house and be my guest as long as you please to stay, for I can never repay your kindness."

The old man shook his head and smiled.

"Alas! I must return to the forest. It is dawn."

"If you must go," said Taiwo, "accept this small reward." And he took out all the coins he had and offered them to the old man.

"No," said his guide, with a strange look. "I am the one to offer you a gift. Young man, I am the spirit of the iroko, and for your gentleness tonight I shall ever watch over this house."

With these words, he thrust into Taiwo's hands his light, and disappeared. The light changed, as Taiwo held it, into a lump of gold, of such great value that Taiwo was a rich man for the rest of his life.

Often he stood in front of the iroko tree, wishing to express his gratitude, but he never saw the old man again, and once or twice, when he caught sight of a light between the trees, he found that it was nothing but the glow-worms who guide travellers falsely into the swamps!

XVII. The Ants and the Serpent

The ants were once building a new city.

They toiled all day long in the hot sun, making rooms and streets, tunnels and porches, and no one thought of taking a rest until the task was finished.

But alas! just when the work was nearing completion, a huge serpent came out of the forest and crawled right through the city of the ants, ruining it, and destroying all the work of the industrious insects.

The chief workers of the ants ran after the serpent, and cried:

"Oh, monster! oh, villain! how could you destroy our work—you, who never create anything beautiful or useful! You must pay us something to make up for the damage you have done with your great heavy body."

The serpent only laughed, as it began to glide up a tree-trunk.

"If you say any more I will come back and crush you all, as well as the mound you call a city!"

"We will have our revenge!" cried the ants, running to and fro, and beginning their toil all over again.

The serpent, lying coiled round a branch, took no notice at all.

That night the ants summoned all their friends and relatives for miles around. Thousands and thousands of ants came marching in a great army to the spot where the great serpent lay asleep in the long grasses.

Silently, swiftly, steadily they marched over all obstacles, and suddenly swarming over the serpent they began to eat him up alive.

The serpent writhed here and there, begging for mercy, but

the ants he had persecuted did not hear his appeal, and though he tied himself into knots and double knots, it was all to no purpose.

When morning came the ants had marched on their way, leaving nothing but the white skeleton of the serpent behind them.

Which shows how the weakest creatures, if banded together, can overcome a strong and dangerous enemy.

XVIII. Tortoise Saves the King

"Oh, King!" said Tortoise, "how many ears have you?"
"Two," replied the King.

"Then listen well with both of them. Here we are, with plenty of food, but outside the city a big army is encamped, and our enemy is only waiting to attack us. And they are very fierce because they are so hungry."

The King replied:

"That is true. I am afraid they may attack at any time, and then what will become of our city? We can only defeat them by a trick, and I have promised to give my daughter to the man who thinks out the best plan."

"Well, King," said Tortoise boldly, "I do not wish to marry your daughter, because I am quite satisfied with Nyanribo, but I have thought of a very good way of defeating the enemy. All I ask is a little basket of provisions from the royal storehouse."

"Is that all? Do you not need money and warriors?"

"Not yet," said Tortoise cautiously, and in a little while he left the town with a small basket of provisions.

He went straight on until he reached a marsh, near which the enemy lay waiting to attack.

Now the sentry and herald of the enemy was a Frog, and he seized his bugle and listened intently when he heard someone approaching.

Tortoise came slowly into sight, carrying his basket, and Frog laughed and threw down the bugle.

"Why, it is Tortoise! What brings you here?"

"Curiosity," returned Tortoise promptly. "I have been told that you are a great runner and jumper, and I did not believe it, so I thought I would come and ask you yourself."

"Has the tale of my wonderful jumping only just reached your ears? You are slow, Tortoise, slow! I am the world's greatest jumper."

Tortoise looked unconvinced.

"It is surprising," he said. "I never thought you in any way remarkable, and yet you say you are famous. . . ."

"Famous?" cried Frog angrily. "This army has chosen me as sentry and herald because I am such a very clever fellow. No one else is fitted for such an important post. I shall certainly become a Chief when the war is over."

"That may be," agreed his visitor, still doubtful. "But, to be convinced, I would have to see an exhibition of your marvellous leaping."

"Oh, of course! I will show you. I can easily jump right across this marsh . . . if I try. But I am not at my best just now, because we are nearly starved to death. As a matter of fact, we shall attack the town to-morrow, and then there will be no hunger again! Even you, Tortoise, would make quite a tasty stew for a hungry warrior. . . ."

Chuckling at his own wit, Frog took a deep breath and sprang into the long grass quite a distance away.

"Did you see me?" he called proudly.

"Not very well," replied Tortoise, who was busy cramming the herald's bugle with the savoury morsels of food he had brought in the basket. "Not very well. Jump again!"

Frog leaped here and there, and then returned, calling: "Did you see me? Did you see me?

"Yes," said Tortoise, picking up his empty basket, "I saw all I came to see, and I am quite satisfied. You are a very wonderful fellow. There is no doubt you will be either a Chief or a King some day!"

"Of course," said Frog, as Tortoise ambled away.

When he arrived, all out of breath, in the King's presence, Tortoise panted:

"Quick! I have arranged everything! Order your warriors to

attack at once. The enemy is encamped behind the marsh, and
we cannot fail to defeat them."

The King gave the necessary orders, and the whole army
quickly advanced towards the marsh.

Frog was alarmed when he saw the warriors advancing, and
he seized the bugle to sound a warning to his friends. To his
astonishment a morsel of food dropped from the bugle into his
mouth, and each time he tried to blow the bugle, the same thing
happened. In the end, hunger overcame discretion, and while
he gobbled up the food, the King's army advanced and fell upon
the enemy without warning, gaining a complete victory.

The warriors returned to the town in triumph, and Tortoise
was the hero of the day.

As for Frog, he ate the contents of his bugle so eagerly that he
burst, and no trace of him was ever found but his bugle.

XIX. Oluronbi's Promise

In a certain village no baby had been born for fourteen years. The women grew idle, as they had no children to care for, and the men, who would have been instructing their sons in the secrets of hunting and wood-craft, as well as in the various occupations of the village, shook their heads sadly over the drowsy silence that reigned where childish prattle and running feet should have made a cheerful and comforting noise.

One night all the men of the village met in a secret grove and discussed the matter. Bada, the drummer, was more vehement than all the rest.

"Alas!" he complained. "I am growing old, and who is there to carry on my work? Shall a stranger from some other village come here with his drum to play for the dancing and to mock at us?"

"Alas!" sighed all the rest.

"There is some evil charm hanging over the village," continued Bada. "Or perhaps the women of the village are not pleasing to the gods. Let us turn them out into the forest."

The rest cried out against such a harsh thought, but the fat goldsmith, Alagbede, said:

"It is true. Our women must be very wicked, since the gods will not trust them to train up little children to bring prosperity to the village. Let us cast them off."

In the end all the men gave their consent to the suggestion, except Sani, the wood-carver, who loved his young wife Oluronbi devotedly. He was a very skilful man, and even the King of the land had praised his carving, for he designed stools

65

supported by the figures of two fighting elephants; and again the shapes of crocodiles, strange birds and beasts of the forest, decorated with the marks of a hot iron, and so lifelike that all were astonished to see them.

Being thus a man of importance in the village, Sani was listened to with respect by the rest, though most of them were older than himself.

"I agree with you, my friends," he declared, "that things are in a very serious state. At the same time, I feel that there is good fortune in store for our village. Let us therefore wait another year before we cast off our wives, and I now pledge you my word that my own wife, Oluronbi, whom I love dearly, shall be the first to go."

After much discussion, the rest agreed, and the meeting came to an end.

But someone reached the village before the men: one of the women, concealed among the tall grasses, had heard every word which had been spoken, and she ran like an antelope to tell her friends what had transpired.

Oh, what sorrowful looks did the women cast upon one another when they heard of the cruel decree of their husbands! But none felt such grief as Oluronbi when the words of Sani the wood-carver were reported.

"Alas! alas!" cried all the women together. "We shall be turned out into the forest to be killed by the leopards and wolves. Alas for Oluronbi, who must be the first to leave!"

Months passed by, and still the spirits of little children refused to come to the village, and the women all wept bitterly when they were alone, and thought with fear of the terrible day which was fast approaching.

One day Oluronbi called all the women together, while the men were out hunting.

"Let us go into the forest and ask the iroko, the magic tree, to help us," she said.

No one had thought of this before, so they all set off at once into the forest, until they came to the magic tree.

The boldest among the women spoke for the rest, and asked the spirit of the tree to help them in their need.

For a long time there was silence, while the unlucky women trembled and wished they had never left the village; when suddenly from the iroko tree came a deep voice like thunder.

"Alas for you, my daughters. There is cause for mourning and sorrow . . . sorrow . . . sorrow. . . . Yet the iroko will aid you. Return home, and if you bring a suitable sacrifice, children shall be given to every one of you."

At this the women wept for joy.

"Oh, great iroko!" cried the wife of Bada the drummer. "I will sacrifice a fat sheep."

"And I a goat," said the wife of fat Alagbede, the goldsmith.

"And I a sucking-pig."

"And I ten young chickens," they said, one after another.

But Oluronbi rejoiced most of all, for she loved her husband dearly.

"Iroko," she cried, "if this is true, I will give you my first child."

Thus happiness came again to the village, and in each hut there was the crowing of children, and the joyful parents went about smiling proudly.

Proudest of all were Sani and Oluronbi with the little girl that was born to them. She was so beautiful, even when she was a tiny infant, that she was called "Layinka," or "Honour-surrounds-me," and when the King passed through the village, he was struck by the sweetness of the little girl, and resolved that she should one day be the bride of his son.

How proudly Oluronbi looked at her little daughter when the King had passed on his way! Then suddenly her promise to the iroko, completely forgotten in her happiness, returned to her memory.

Trembling with fear, Oluronbi held the baby in her arms and thought of her terrible promise. But she could not bear to sacrifice her sweet little daughter to the magic tree, and hoped that with the gifts of fat sheep and goats, choice fruits and ornaments of gold laid at the foot of the tree by the other women, the iroko would be content.

However, for a long time she was afraid to go near the magic tree, and meanwhile her daughter Layinka grew rapidly to be a beautiful and amiable child, so that her parents were very proud of her.

After a while Oluronbi forgot all about her promise to the iroko, and went with the other women into the forest as before. One day, walking alone, she thoughtlessly passed by the iroko tree, singing as she went:

> "Layinka, my beautiful child,
> Thou art thy mother's joy."

Evening came, and in the village there was no trace of Oluronbi. All the villagers were alarmed, but especially Sani the wood-carver, who ran from hut to hut trying to find his wife.

She could not be discovered, and after a sleepless night Sani went at daybreak into the forest, where Oluronbi had last been seen. Here again his search met with no reward, and towards evening he turned his steps sorrowfully back to the village.

In the shade of the iroko tree he sat down for a little while to rest. There was a flutter of wings in the leafy branches, and a little brown bird appeared and began to sing these strange words:

> "Everyone promised a goat, a goat!
> Everyone promised a sheep, a sheep!
> But Oluronbi promised her child, her child;
> Her child as sweet as the red palm-oil!
> Poor Oluronbi!
> Here sits she,
> Confined to the boughs of iroko tree."

Several times this song was repeated, and at length Sani realized that the little brown bird could be none other than Oluronbi herself!

He sprang to his feet, but the bird disappeared.

When he reached the village, Sani related what had happened and soon learned the meaning of the song, for all the women confessed how they had gone to the iroko tree for help and had promised various gifts. Nobody was surprised that poor Oluronbi had found it impossible to sacrifice her pretty baby, and it was evident that the iroko tree had seized the unfortunate woman as she passed by, and changed her into a bird.

Sani and the Magic Tree. *Page 70.*

Sani sat all night by the door of his hut, thinking how he might rescue his wife from her sad fate, and at last an idea came to him.

As soon as it was light he chose a fine piece of wood and his sharpest tools, and began to carve. For three days he carved away in secret, and at the end of that time he had completed the figure of a baby, so lifelike that all who saw it believed it at first to be a real child.

He wrapped this wooden baby in a handsome blue cloth and hung a small gold chain about its neck. Then he set off once more to the forest.

In the branches of the iroko tree the little brown bird was still singing plaintively.

Sani laid the wooden baby on the ground and cried:

> "Iroko! Iroko!
> Take up Oluronbi's child.
> Here is the child,
> As red as palm-oil,
> As sweet as a paw-paw!
> Oh, take the child from me.
> The small brown bird set free!"

The branches of the iroko creaked and swayed and suddenly bent down to snatch up the wooden baby, which disappeared in the midst of the thick leaves.

And before Sani the wood-carver stood his weeping wife.

"Alas! alas! husband," she cried. "I would rather have remained for ever a poor brown bird than that our beautiful Layinka, who was to wed the King's son, should be given up to the cruel iroko!"

Without any explanation Sani led her swiftly from the forest, and when they reached the entrance of their hut . . . there sat little Layinka, laughing happily and playing with her wooden toys.

Sani then explained the trick he had played on the iroko tree, and warned Oluronbi never again to make a promise to anybody without first asking his advice.

Layinka grew up to be a sweet and lovable girl, and in time wedded the prince and lived happily ever after, to the joy and satisfaction of her parents.

XX. The Head

There once was a strange country where the inhabitants had heads but no bodies. The Heads moved about the ground by taking little jumps, but they never went far, because it was such a slow way of travelling.

One of the Heads grew restless and desired to see the world, so one day he set off and travelled as fast as he could over the bumpy ground to the border of the next kingdom. At this spot a hunter's cottage stood, and seeing a woman in the doorway, the Head called out:

"I pray you, friend, can you lend me a body? I desire to see the world, and this method of travelling is too slow for me."

The woman took pity on the Head, and lent him the body of her young servant boy. After that the Head went along a little faster, but he began to grow weary and was glad indeed to reach a small village.

Under a large shady tree a young man lay drowsing, away from the heat of the sun, and the Head approached him.

"I pray you, friend," said the Head, "can you lend me a pair of arms? I desire to see the world, but I should be much better off if I had arms."

The young man, who was of a lazy disposition, thought for a moment before replying:

"Well, I would gladly lend you my arms, but I shall need them two days from now, when I have promised to help my father on the farm."

"I require your arms only for one day," returned the Head

71

eagerly. "To-morrow evening I will gladly bring them back to you, if you will do me this great kindness."

The young man then consented to lend his arms, and the Head set off once more, helping himself along with his new hands, and he soon covered quite a good distance.

Towards evening, however, his body began to ache and his hands to smart, from the roughness of the road, and he therefore stooped at a river-side, near some fishermen's huts, and asked if anyone could lend him a pair of legs.

"I desire to see the world," explained the Head, "but what use am I without legs? With legs one can do a thousand things!"

One of the fishermen agreed to lend the Head his legs just for one day, and so with a complete and handsome form the Head took long strides in the direction of a town which he could see in the distance. As he approached, he heard the sound of music, and on reaching the town he found all the inhabitants gathered in a certain place to watch the dancing of young maidens about to become betrothed.

One maiden, more beautiful and graceful than the rest, received all the applause, and as he gazed at her, the Head fell instantly in love.

When she finished her dance and disappeared from sight, the Head lost all interest in the sights of the town, which he had travelled so far to see, and he spent the whole night in strolling miserably to and fro, and wondering if he would ever behold the beautiful maiden again.

The next morning he sought her early among the groups of girls chattering in the market-place or busy washing clothes in the river. She was nowhere to be found.

In despair the Head was just about to return to his own country, when he saw the maiden, with whose charms he was so overpowered, walking along with a large calabash of pineapples on her head, for she was one of the fruit-sellers, and had been selling fruit in other parts of the town all morning.

On the pretence that he wished to buy pineapples, the Head approached her and said:

"Beautiful maiden, what is your name?"

"My name," she replied, in girlish confusion, "is Aduke."

"Then, Aduke," said the love-smitten Head, "you are the most beautiful person I have ever seen, and I am entirely overcome by the power of your charms."

"Alas, noble youth! You are certainly mocking me!" cried the girl in astonishment.

"Indeed, such an intention is far from my thoughts," he replied earnestly. "I have spent the whole night thinking about you, and if you will consent to become my bride and return with me to my own country, I shall be as happy as the lion, king of animals, who, having no rival, secures the richest of all the prizes in his hunting."

Aduke could not help admiring his tall stature, graceful bearing, and smooth words, and therefore answered:

"Is your country far from here? I should be very lonely."

"My country is but one day's journey hence, and I promise you that any time you desire to see your friends you may return here for one day's visit, but only if you will agree to stay with me always like a faithful wife, whatever happens."

After a great deal of persuasion, the maiden's heart was won, and before evening the marriage was performed, and dancing and feasting continued long into the night at the house of the bride's parents.

As soon as it was dawn, the Head was anxious to depart, and tearing the weeping girl from her parents and friends, he bade her somewhat harshly to make ready for the journey. Shortly afterwards the pair left the town together, Aduke casting sorrowful glances behind her as her home grew more and more distant.

"If you are always looking back," said the Head sadly, "I shall feel sure that you do not love me."

"Indeed," replied his bride, "I regret leaving my home, but I will stay with you always like a faithful wife, whatever happens."

After walking for some time, they reached a river, with a few fishermen's huts on its banks. Here the Head stopped, and to the horror of his bride removed his legs and gave them to one of the fishermen who sat mending his nets in front of a hut.

"Have you seen the world, friend?" asked the fisherman.

"Yes, and your legs have won me a beautiful bride," replied

the Head; and as he moved forward on his hands and body, Aduke burst into tears and followed him weeping.

They had not been progressing thus for many hours when they reached a village. Here they partook of food and drink, for Aduke was by this time faint with weariness and bitterly regretted her foolishness in listening to the fine words of the stranger.

When they were sufficiently rested, and were about to proceed on their way, the Head called out to a youth who lay under the shade of a large breadfruit tree. The youth recognized him and came forward.

"Friend, here are your arms," said the Head.

"I am very glad to have them back again," replied the youth. "I must hasten to my father's fields, or I shall receive a good beating for my laziness. Have you seen the world now, friend?"

"Yes," said the Head as before, "and your arms have won me this beautiful bride."

Weeping more bitterly than ever, Aduke followed her husband as he moved very slowly along the road.

Towards evening they reached a small hunter's cottage. Here a woman stood in the doorway, and on seeing the Head she seemed very glad and hastened forward, exclaiming:

"We have had such an uproar in the house. My servant has been demanding his body the whole time, and has given us no peace. I suppose you have seen the world now, friend."

"Yes, indeed, and your servant's body has won me this beautiful bride."

When she saw that her husband was nothing more nor less than a head, Aduke ran forward and walked in front of him, as she could not bear to look upon him.

What was her surprise, therefore, on reaching his home, to find that all the inhabitants of the country were in a similar condition.

However, she could not grow accustomed to the strangeness of seeing her husband and his friends bounding along the ground without either body or limbs, and even after living in the country of the Heads for a very long time, she did nothing but weep and regret the pleasant existence she had left behind.

At length, realizing that she would soon die of grief if she continued in this manner, she approached her husband and addressed him as follows:

"It is now a long time, husband, since you brought me here from my own country, and even if I live to be a hundred I shall never grow accustomed to the strange life in this place. I have forgiven you for the cruel trick you played on me, when I promised to accompany you and to remain faithfully with you for ever; but I must ask you one small favour, without which I can no longer exist here with you!"

"What is the favour?" asked her husband, feeling sad and anxious.

"I desire you to cut off my body and limbs, so that I may be a Head like one of you, and no longer feel my loneliness here in a strange country."

Joyfully the Head consented, and Aduke became a Head. After this she ceased weeping, and became happy and contented among her husband's people.

Now and again she put on her body and visited her parents for a day. Her husband never accompanied her, and at the end of the day she always returned dutifully home and became a Head again, living thus to a very great age, and being renowned throughout the country of the Heads for her beauty, wisdom, and virtue.

The moral of this story is, that where we cannot alter our circumstances, it is the wisest course to adapt ourselves to them.

XXI. Tortoise Tricks the Lion

"Oh, King!" cried Tortoise one day, "how many ears have you?"

"I still have two, and you may be sure they are both impatient to hear what you are about to say," replied the King, for when Tortoise saluted him in this manner, he always had something exciting to relate.

"Well," said Tortoise, "I have heard that on the edge of the great desert which lies to the north of Your Majesty's kingdom, there dwells a Lion—a very ferocious monster—who, not content with being King of the Desert, desires to be King of the Forest as well, and who is now marching upon villages in the bush and eating everybody he meets."

The King trembled, and the members of his Court cast frightened looks here and there, as if they feared the Lion might walk in upon them at any moment.

"Do not speak of it, Chief Tortoise!" said the King hastily. "It is a very terrible thing, and has cost me several sleepless nights. But what is there to be done? This Lion is afraid of nothing. His roar causes trees to fall and the elephant and leopard to hide for safety when they hear it. Even a dozen men cannot capture the King of the Desert, for he knocks them down with his mighty paws and devours them one after another, and the spears they throw are turned aside from his yellow body by some powerful charm which no one can discover."

"Yes," said Tortoise boldly, "I have heard all this, and a lot more besides, which I will not trouble to repeat, as it would only cause you more sleepless nights. Yes, I have heard; but I am not afraid. True, I am not very strong, but I am cunning, and by cunning I shall outwit this terrible beast and so rid the forest of a dangerous enemy."

"Alas, my little champion!" exclaimed the King. "With one blow of his paw the Lion will smash your shell to pieces. How can you harm such a creature?"

Tortoise waved his head knowingly from side to side, and replied:

"There is a proverb, 'One may enter the house and yet not enter the heart,' but I mean to enter both."

"You speak in riddles, Tortoise, but if you return alive, I will give you a palace to live in!" declared the King. And soon afterwards Tortoise set off on his long journey to the north.

After he had travelled for many days, he came to a village almost at the edge of the forest, where the people told him that the Lion was not far away, and that they expected him at any moment to run into the village and eat them all up.

"I seem to have arrived just in time!" declared Tortoise. "I have been sent by the King, and I am going to save you all from this horrible beast."

"Alas, brave Tortoise! How can you hope to defeat the Lion, when he has been known to devour, one after another, ten mighty warriors who rushed out with their spears to slay him?"

"I carry no spear," replied Tortoise modestly. "I am no doubt a poor, weak creature, but I shall defeat the Lion by cunning."

Despite all protests, Tortoise set off to find the Lion, whose name was Kiniyun. He walked boldly through the forest in the direction pointed out by the villagers, until he came to Kiniyun's house, which was a dark cave surrounded and almost buried by grasses and creepers.

Kiniyun was away killing people in some village, so Tortoise went into the cave and waited in the darkest corner for the Lion's return.

Late in the evening, when it was very dark and gloomy inside the cave, Kiniyun came back, and Tortoise heard his feet padding about the cave, as if he suspected the presence of a stranger.

"Friend," said Tortoise at once. "I have lost my way in the forest, and I came into this cave for shelter. Who are you?"

The Lion began to roar in a very terrifying manner.

"Who am I? I am Kiniyun, King of the Desert and of the Forest, and I mean to eat you up."

"Great King," said Tortoise in his small, high voice, "I should be a very tasteless mouthful, and I am sure that so great a monarch has no need of such a miserable banquet."

"True enough," said Kiniyun. "But I make a point of devouring everybody, and why should I make an exception of you, who—to judge by your voice and smell, for I cannot see you— are a most insignificant creature."

"Ah!" said Tortoise. "It is just because of that that I feel you ought to spare me! I am far too insignificant to harm you. Besides, if you eat everybody you meet, you must feel very lonely, and I think we could spend a pleasant evening together."

"Very well," agreed Kiniyun. "We may as well enjoy a little conversation—but I warn you, I may eat you all the same, if the feeling comes over me."

"Let us hope it will not!" murmured Tortoise fervently, and he came a little forward.

The two animals sat down side by side and began to talk about the forest. Tortoise told the Lion funny stories about the cowardly leopard, and the cowardly wolf, and the cowardly elephant, and the cowardly giraffe, until tears rolled down Kiniyun's face, and he shook the cave with his laughter.

"Ha! ha! ha! What cowards there are in the forest! It is time you had a real king like myself to reign over you."

"If there are any of us left when you have finished eating!" observed Tortoise, and the Lion went into another fit of laughter.

"No doubt," pursued his guest, "you do not fear anything in the world?"

"Certainly not! And do you fear anything?"

"Why, yes!" admitted Tortoise frankly. "I confess that I cannot bear to see a crab, and I detest the boa-constrictor. But let us make a fire, for the night is cold . . . and besides, I would like to see you!"

"Oh no," said Kiniyun hastily. "I won't have a fire in here. Why, it is dangerous!"

Tortoise and the Lion. *Page 77.*

However, Tortoise gave him no peace, and persisted in his demand for a fire.

"Surely the King of the Forest and of the Scorching Desert is not afraid of fire!" he said mockingly.

The Lion repeated indignantly that he was afraid of nothing, and at last consented to have a fire—but not inside the cave.

So they both went outside and made a fire and sat down beside it. But Tortoise noticed that the Lion kept at a good distance from the fire, and watched the flames suspiciously out of the corner of his eye.

"Dear me! What a cold night it is!" said Tortoise, pretending to shiver. "I have never felt so cold at the end of the rainy season before. I will put some more branches on the fire."

"No!" cried Lion. "Fire is dangerous. This is quite big enough—I can't allow you to add any more branches!"

"Ha! ha!" thought Tortoise inside his head. "Lion is afraid of fire!" But aloud he only remarked: "Yes, you are right. Fire is dangerous. Have you heard about the great fire which happened a hundred years ago?"

"No," said Kiniyun, trembling and moving still further away. "Tell me about it at once, before I eat you. I begin to feel hungry again."

"Well," Tortoise made haste to reply, "a hundred years ago in a village not far from this spot, a small fire was left burning at night when everybody was asleep. And suddenly the dry grass caught fire, and then the shrubs caught fire, and soon even the tallest trees were a mass of flames, and everyone perished."

"What a gruesome tale!" cried Kiniyun, his teeth chattering and his mane shaking with fear. "But, of course, that was a hundred years ago, long before you or I were born, and I don't expect it will occur again."

Tortoise chuckled.

"Not occur again? Why, the forest is on fire at this very minute!"

Kiniyun gave a roar and sprang up into the air.

"On fire? Where? When? How? Why?"

"Where?" replied Tortoise. "At the next village from here, in the direction of the south. When? This evening as I came through. How? By the carelessness of the Chief's wife, who overturned a jar of oil while she was cooking the supper. Why? Because the forest is a dangerous place to live in."

Lion ran here and there in great terror, sniffing the air for fire, and when his back was turned, Tortoise quickly seized one of the flaming branches, and threw it into the grass beside the cave, and all in a moment the dry grass began to blaze and crackle.

"Look! look!" cried Tortoise. "Did I not tell you that the forest is on fire?"

But Lion, with another roar, set off as hard as he could go towards the desert. Tortoise at once put out the fire and hastened back to the village, where he beat loudly on a drum and summoned all the people together.

"Light a great fire in the centre of the village," he commanded. "Do not waste time asking me questions. I will tell you all about it later."

The villagers obeyed without hesitation, and made a great fire of wood, so that the night soon appeared as light as day.

Meanwhile Kiniyun had stopped running, thinking that after all there might be no fire in the forest.

"Perhaps this is a plot to get rid of me!" he thought. But as he turned back, he saw far away the terrible flames of the fire which the villagers had made. After this the Lion was quite convinced, and he went off at once right to the edge of the desert, and decided never to go into the forest again, even when he felt very hungry.

The villagers were extremely grateful for what Tortoise had done, and when he departed he advised them to light fires every evening outside the village, to scare away Kiniyun or any of his family who might come prowling near.

After many days Tortoise again reached the town where the King lived with his Court. But news travels fast, and when he came to the end of his journey, the King had already heard all about the defeat of Kiniyun. He had prepared a splendid palace, with a great number of slaves, and in it Tortoise and his wife Nyanribo lived happily for many years.

XXII. War About a Goat

Once upon a time there lived a woman named Aina, who was very fond of animals.

She had a small house but a very large garden, and in the garden she kept a great number of pets, including hens and ducks, a goat and a cow, a little leopard and a dog, and even lizards and snakes.

Every animal which strayed into her garden was sure to be welcome, and after some time Aina became well known in the town for her pets, which followed her about when she left the house.

But of all the animals, the one she liked the best was the goat, to whom she talked as if it were a human being, and who was, in fact, treated far better than any of the other pets.

Now one day a man from the next town passed by Aina's house. The man was called Ayo, and he was very hungry, and had no money to buy provisions. In Aina's garden he heard the noise of hens clucking, a dog barking, a leopard snarling, and a goat bleating.

He was so much astonished that he climbed on to the wall and looked down into the garden.

He saw all the animals walking about there in a very contented way. He had felt hungry before, but now he was ravenous.

"To think of such plump chickens wasting in this garden!" thought Ayo. "I will steal a chicken and take it home."

Then he changed his mind and said again:

"To think of such good milk wasting here! I will milk the cow and relieve my thirst."

But when he saw the goat, which was so plump and well cared for, he changed his mind again and exclaimed:

"To think of such a fine goat bleating here all day long! Really I must take the goat home with me!"

So he a found means of entering the garden, and tied a rope to the goat's neck, by which he led her as fast as he could along the road to the next town. But the goat did not care to go so fast, and he soon nibbled through the rope and ran away, leaving the man to walk on with the rope in his hand, and to arrive home very disappointed at having lost his supper.

Now when Aina found that her goat had disappeared, she at once suspected Ayo, whom she had seen peeping over her garden wall. She ran to the King and told him that her goat had been stolen by a man from the next town; and the King was very angry, and sent his best warriors to attack the other town and bring back the goat.

But the people of the next town were good fighters, and they too sent out their best warriors, and so war began.

Meanwhile the goat had returned home and was bleating in Aina's garden just as before. When the news of this reached the King, he at once commanded his warriors to cease fighting and return to the town, which they soon did.

But the people of the other town were angry at having been attacked for no reason, and they in their turn came to attack the King, so that the war began all over again.

Seeing how the matter stood, the goat, who was far wiser than most goats, thought it best to leave Aina's garden, and he ran away and hid once more in the woods.

Aina hastened back to the King, weeping, and said:

"Your Majesty, I am a poor woman, but I still have to suffer because of the wickedness of that rascal Ayo. My pet goat has been stolen again, and who else would dare to perform such a deed but a man from the next town?"

This time the King was very angry, and the war was continued fiercely.

Thus no doubt it might have gone on for ever, if the people of the other town had not realized how foolish it was to fight so hard because of a goat.

So they sent messengers to the King, with the following declaration:

"The woman Aina says that her goat has been stolen by a man from our town. We will gather together all the goats in the town, and if Aina can pick out her own goat from among them, it shall be returned to her, and a large sum of money besides."

But they thought craftily that Aina would never be able to find her own goat among so many all alike, and they were quite sure that she would have to admit that the pet goat had not been stolen at all!

This would certainly have been the case, if the goat, who was still hiding in the woods, had not heard of the declaration, and, being so much wiser than other goats, immediately set off for the town where a great muster of goats was being held. He took his place among them without anyone noticing him, and soon afterwards Aina came with an escort from the King, to pick out her pet.

Alas! When the poor woman saw dozens and dozens of goats in rows before her, she despaired of ever finding her own, and walked up and down before them in great sorrow, not troubling to study them, for they all appeared exactly alike.

Now the people of the town began to smile and to whisper: "The victory is ours! The King will have to pay us a large sum as compensation, because he fought against us for no reason at all."

Suddenly one goat came out from among the rest and went bleating up to Aina. Looking down, Aina recognized her pet, and flung her arms about the wise animal's neck.

After this there could be no doubt that the goat had been stolen, and Aina departed in triumph with her pet and a large sum of money to console her for what she had suffered.

As they walked along the road, they passed by the wood, and in the wood Ayo was hiding, for he was afraid of being punished for the theft. As the goat went by, Ayo hissed:

"Hateful animal! You have ruined me! I wish I had choked you that night with my rope, instead of leading you by it!"

But the wise goat of course pretended not to hear!

XXIII. The Elephant and the Rhinoceros

Tortoise had nothing to do! He wandered along the bank of the river, looking for some means of passing the time. At last he saw the Rhinoceros, splashing about noisily in the water, and looking very cool and pleased with himself.

Tortoise called out to him "Karo!" which means "Good-morning!" The Rhinoceros said nothing at all.

"Ill-mannered creature!" thought Tortoise crossly, as he went on.

Some distance away, the Elephant stood under a tree, lazily breaking off leaves with his trunk.

"Karo!" said Tortoise hopefully.

"Run away, silly Tortoise! Pop into your shell and don't come interfering with me!" said the Elephant.

Tortoise walked further on, wondering why everybody was so rude to-day. When he had walked a little way he retired into his shell, and thought how to pay back the Elephant and the Rhinoceros for their bad treatment of him.

An idea soon came into his mind, for he was always ready for mischief. He found a long piece of rope, and then hurried back to the Elephant.

"Karo!" said Tortoise. "Karo! Karo! Karo! Why won't you say good-morning to me? I think you are very rude as well as weak."

"Weak?" grunted the Elephant. "Who said I was weak?"

"The Rhinoceros said so," replied Tortoise promptly. "He has been telling everybody that you are a weakling and that you have no strength in your trunk."

"What an insult!" said the Elephant indignantly, stamping with his great feet. "I can uproot big trees with my trunk."

"Is that so?" said Tortoise. "Then you can easily prove your strength. I will tie one end of this rope to your trunk and the other end to a log which I saw floating in the river. If you can pull the log out of the river, then you are strong."

The Elephant laughed at this simple test, and readily allowed Tortoise to tie the rope to his trunk.

Then Tortoise went to the edge of the river and called out to the Rhinoceros, who was dozing peacefully in the water:

"Karo! Wake up and listen to me! The Elephant has been say-ing . . . But you are not listening. I will go away and tell some-one else instead!"

The Rhinoceros opened his eyes, blew a great puff of water from his mouth, and said:

"Good-morning, Tortoise! How impatient you are! What has my friend the Elephant been saying?"

"Your friend?" laughed the mischief-maker. "Your friend has been telling everybody what a lazy, dirty, weak creature you are! He says that you have no strength in your horn, and that you could not even knock down a frog."

"A frog?" spluttered the Rhinoceros. "What an insult! Who is the Elephant, after all, to spread insults about me, when I am far stronger than he is, and can knock down not only frogs but even trees . . . if I wish. Only, of course, it is much more com-fortable to lie here in the nice warm mud and sleep."

"And while you lie there, everyone says that you are a weak-ling! Why don't you show them how strong you are? Do you see this rope? I have fastened the other end of it to a tree. Let me tie this end round your horn, and if you can pull the tree down, then no one will deny that you are strong."

The Rhinoceros agreed, and allowed the rope to be tied to his horn.

Then Tortoise gave a signal to the Elephant and the Rhinoceros. They both began to pull the rope, and each was sur-prised to find what a great weight there seemed to be at the other end. They pulled and pulled, while Tortoise stood behind a tree and laughed at them both.

The tugging went on all day long, but the Elephant found that he could not pull out what he thought was a log in the river, and in the same way Rhinoceros could not succeed in uprooting his tree.

At last, when it was evening and almost time for darkness to begin, the Elephant stopped pulling for a little while, and went down to the water to have a drink. At the very same moment the Rhinoceros stopped pulling too, and came up on to the river bank to rest.

They were both very angry, but, as they met, the Elephant said: "What are you doing with a rope tied to your horn?"

And the Rhinoceros said: "What are *you* doing with a rope tied round your trunk?"

Then it suddenly struck them that Tortoise must have played them a trick, and they were both overwhelmed with shame. At last the Elephant said fiercely:

"Where is that rascal Tortoise? I will trample on him with my feet."

"Yes," said the Rhinoceros angrily, "and I will pierce him with my horn!"

They set off at once to look for Tortoise, but you may be sure he was nowhere to be found, and to this very hour, he is still keeping out of their way.

XXIV. The Abyss of Ajaye

Once upon a time there was a brave and powerful King called Olofin, who ruled over an island called Iddo Island at the top of a very long and very wide lagoon.

Young, strong, and handsome, Olofin searched everywhere for a maiden suitable to be his wife. But alas! Neighbouring princesses were either too dull or too ugly to please the young King, until at last it came to his ears that in a remote country there dwelt a chief named Oluwo, who had a most beautiful daughter. The rumour ran that this princess excelled in wit and accomplishments above all other women in the land, and when he learnt this, Olofin departed at once to behold with his own eyes the possessor of so many charms.

Clad in the richest raiment, attended by many slaves, and bearing presents of great value, he left Iddo Island and travelled through wild forest and marsh until he reached the town where the remarkable princess lived.

His arrival, heralded by the drummers, caused a great stir in the town, and Chief Oluwo himself hastened to meet him with a guard of picked warriors, all of them giants at least eight feet tall.

"Welcome, King Olofin!" said Oluwo heartily. "To what do we owe the honour of your visit?"

"I am here," declared Olofin, coming to the point at once, "to seek the hand of your daughter in marriage, because I have heard glowing reports of her beauty, her wit, and her womanly excellence. For three years I have been seeking such a bride, and I am overjoyed at the thought that my quest is ended."

Oluwo assured him that he would be delighted to give his daughter to so illustrious a suitor, and they went into the palace of the Chief, where Olofin presented his host with some of the gifts he had brought with him.

Just as Chief Oluwo was admiring a wonderful spear with head of gold and shaft of ivory, Olofin beheld a maiden of dazzling beauty peeping at him from behind a tree in the courtyard. Her hair was long and like a cloud, her eyes glistened like stars, and her pouting red lips disclosed teeth quite undistinguishable from the finest pearls. Heavy golden bangles encircled her slender wrists and ankles.

As he gazed upon her, King Olofin fell violently in love. Darting forward, he seized the maiden's hand and fell on his knees before her.

"My princess!" he exclaimed. "How long have I sought you! And how inadequate were the praises which I heard concerning you! Well may your beauty be renowned throughout the land, for you are surely the most beautiful woman in the world!"

The maiden withdrew her hand, and covered her face in confusion.

"Alas, noble King!" she replied. "She whom you seek is within the palace. I am only her younger sister Ajaye."

So saying, she disappeared, and the bewildered King returned to his companions, thinking that the elder princess must be very beautiful indeed, if Ajaye, the younger and unknown, were so alluring.

He expressed this feeling to Oluwo, who replied hastily:

"Take no notice of that girl; she is a crocodile. My elder daughter is the one you must love. Let us enter, and she shall be brought before you."

They entered the inner part of the palace, and King Olofin was given a seat of honour upon a divan covered with velvet cloths. He awaited with impatience the entrance of the beautiful princess, but she absolutely refused to appear!

Chief Oluwo was much embarrassed by this reply to his summons, and he went himself to fetch his daughter. But she still refused to show herself to her noble suitor, and not until late in the evening was she led into the room.

King Olofin leaned eagerly forward to catch the first glimpse of the renowned princess, but what he saw filled him with amazement and anger.

The princess advanced awkwardly, for she was as fat and clumsy as a rhinoceros. Her hair was scanty, her features were repulsive, and indeed Olofin could not discover a single charm about her.

"Daughter," said Chief Oluwo, trembling before her, "behold the princely suitor who has come to carry you away to his own country, leaving us desolate!"

For a moment the young King was speechless, but he knew that unless he spoke at once, he would certainly be obliged to marry this hideous creature.

"There has been some mistake!" he exclaimed. "This is not the lady who was described to me, and I cannot marry her."

On hearing this the princess started up, enraged, and cast upon Olofin a look of extreme fury as she uttered these venomous words:

"You have scorned me, foolish Olofin. You will choose another in my place. But by the power of the charm which I wear round my neck, may she whom you wed be headless!"

So saying, she rushed from the room, but not before the King had perceived that she wore, suspended on a gold chain, a very powerful charm, by which she forced her father and all his people to obey and admire her.

But Olofin was a fearless man, and he himself wore a powerful charm, so that he laughed at her threat, and made many apologies to Oluwo for what had happened.

Then he returned sadly to his own country of Iddo Island, where the people had prepared to welcome his bride with great festivities. They were disappointed when he returned alone, and began to whisper that the great King would never find a princess worthy to be his wife.

All this time Olofin was haunted by the memory of the beautiful maiden Ajaye, whom he had seen in the courtyard, and his love for her became so great that he felt he could not live without her. He resolved to undertake once more the perilous journey to the country of the Chief Oluwo, in order to see her. This time he took with him only one of his counsellors and a dozen well-armed slaves. After many adventures King Olofin and his little company reached Oluwo's town. He was astonished to hear of their arrival, and hastened to meet them.

The young King did not delay in stating the reason for his visit.

"Last time," he said, "I came with pomp and a large retinue to win the hand of a renowned princess, but this time I come humbly and without display to seek as my bride a little maiden whom I saw in your courtyard."

"My daughter Ajaye!" cried Oluwo. "Alas, King Olofin! She is a child, and without any accomplishments; a foolish maiden, unworthy to be your bride."

"On the contrary," said Olofin firmly, "out of all the women in the world, she is the one I have chosen. She is indeed as beautiful as a young leopard, as graceful as an antelope, and I cannot live without her."

"Have you so soon forgotten the prophecy of the one whom you slighted?" asked Chief Oluwo, trembling. "I cannot bear to think that Ajaye should some day be headless!"

But Olofin would not listen to such words, and to cut a long story short, he left the town soon afterwards with the beautiful Ajaye beside him.

Loud were the acclamations with which the people of Iddo Island greeted the young Queen, who was soon beloved by all for her beauty and sweetness. She bore thirty-two sons to gladden Olofin's heart, and many years passed pleasantly for them all.

Now it happened after a very long time that a powerful enemy of King Olofin sent warriors in war canoes to Iddo Island, and they would certainly have conquered and slain everybody but for the charm which Olofin wore, which protected him in battle, and made him always victorious.

When the enemy found they could not win by fighting, they resolved to use cunning, and a spy was sent to Iddo Island, disguised as a hunter with leopard-skins and elephant-tusks to sell. In this disguise he went to King Olofin's palace, and returned there day after day until at last one morning he saw the Queen, Ajaye, walking in the courtyard.

"Magic charms!" called the spy boldly. "I have charms made from snake-skins and from the teeth of crocodiles. I have the fur of a baby leopard, and the tusks of an elephant two hundred years old!"

Ajaye was curious to see these wonders, and allowed the hunter to display his wares before her. He told her such wonderful stories of his adventures in the forest that she listened for a long time. When no one was near, the spy whispered to her:

"Alas! My charms are all worthless compared with the one which protects the life of your husband, King Olofin!"

Ajaye smiled with pleasure, for she loved Olofin dearly, and was proud of his success in battle.

"And yet," continued the crafty spy, "everybody says that the King guards his charm very closely, and that not even the Queen has seen it."

"That is false!" said Ajaye quickly. "The charm is a ring which the King wears upon his right hand."

The hunter professed to be much astonished, but said: "That may be so. But it is certainly true that the King never allows anyone, not even his Queen, to touch the charm."

"That also is false!" replied foolish Ajaye. "The King trusts me, and allows me to touch the ring whenever I wish. To prove it, I will bring the charm to show you, if you return at this hour tomorrow morning."

The spy went joyfully away, and that night, while Olofin slept, Ajaye softly removed the ring from his hand and hid it in her garments, and the next morning she showed it triumphantly to the hunter.

As she held up the ring, the spy quickly snatched it from her and fled. Realizing how she had been tricked, Ajaye fell fainting to the ground, and so allowed the spy to leave the palace and return to his friends.

Now when Olofin discovered that he had lost his ring, he was filled with dread, but, of course, he never suspected that Ajaye could have stolen it from him, and the poor Queen was so overcome with shame and fear that she dared not tell him the truth. The slaves searched in vain through the palace; no trace of the ring could be found.

And the very next day the enemy came with their long war canoes to attack Iddo Island. But now that the charm was lost, the King was no longer victorious, and during the day he himself was taken prisoner, and carried away bound and helpless in one of the canoes.

With what despair and regret did Ajaye mourn that night, afraid to confide the truth even to her sons, who tried in vain to comfort her.

Meanwhile at Benin City, the town of his enemies, King Olofin was shut up in a building without any entrance, and surrounded by high walls, to die of starvation. At the end of the third day, the building was opened, and out walked Olofin as strong as ever.

His enemies were astonished, and their King ordered the prisoner to be brought before him. Gazing upon the proud and silent King, he exclaimed:

"Olofin, I see that your charm lies not only in the ring which you used to wear on your hand, for you have lived three days without food or water and appear as strong as before! Your wife Ajaye should have confided the whole secret to my spy!"

Olofin remained proudly silent, but his heart broke when he heard of the treachery of his beloved Ajaye. Throughout his misfortunes he had never ceased to think of her, and to believe her the most perfect woman in the world. Even when the King of Benin City declared him free and promised to send him back to Iddo Island in a large canoe, he remained silent, and left the town without uttering a word.

But his heart burned with sorrow and anger that Ajaye should have betrayed him, and immediately on reaching Iddo Island once more, he ordered her to be beheaded.

While his people rejoiced at his return, Olofin suffered the pangs of deepest sorrow, and suddenly desiring to hear the true story from his wife's lips, before he finally condemned her, he rushed to the palace. But he arrived too late! Ajaye had already been beheaded, and her beautiful body lay lifeless on the ground. Yet so great had been their love, that as he gazed, weeping, upon her, the headless body of Ajaye rose from the ground and ran towards him, holding out beseeching hands.

Then the King remembered the prophecy of her slighted sister—"May she whom you wed be headless!"—and seizing Ajaye's hands, he forgave her, repenting only the rashness of his command.

For a long time the body of Ajaye lived in the palace, moving about just as before, until one day a hunter came to the palace gates, with the skins of wild animals which he had slain.

"I have the skin of a boa-constrictor two thousand years old, and the tail of a baby elephant!" cried the hunter, seeking purchasers for his wares.

But as the words were uttered, a mournful cry was heard all over Iddo Island, and the unhappy Queen ran down to the sea and there was drowned.

King Olofin, stricken with grief, lived on for some time, and then he too, despairing of his great loneliness, cast himself into the sea at the same spot, which bears to this day the name of "The Abyss of Ajaye."

XXV. The Magician's Parrot

In a certain town there were two magicians, who were not very friendly towards one another. The first magician was called Oke, and the second Ata.

Oke spent his time discovering the secrets of the animals and the birds of the forest, while Ata concocted in his hut strange charms from herbs and flowers, and sold the charms to bring success and happiness to those who bought them.

Now it happened one day that the King fell ill of a mysterious disease which had never been seen before, and as he seemed likely to die, he sent for the two magicians and promised to give a large reward to whichever of them could succeed in curing him.

The two magicians went home, and Ata began brewing herbs and crushing petals and wild berries in the darkness of his hut, while Oke, who knew nothing about such things, wandered despairingly in the forest, wishing that he could find some means of winning the reward promised by the King.

Now Oke had a clever grey parrot, which he took from the forest when it was very young, and taught to speak and to understand his conversation.

As he strolled among the trees, the grey parrot was perched on his shoulder.

"Alas!" said the magician aloud. "How can I hope to cure the King? I know nothing about herbs, whereas Ata is at this very moment preparing a charm which will restore the King to good health."

"Send me!" said the grey parrot. "Send me! Send me!"

The magician was struck by these words, and decided to send the parrot to the rival's house to learn what he could about the charm.

That evening when Ata was busy over his fire with a large pot of herbs, a grey parrot flew in through the door and perched on his shoulder. At first Ata was startled, but he knew nothing about animals or birds and decided that the parrot must be a good omen for his success. He therefore allowed the bird to stay with him, and fed it with corn.

The next evening Oke, the other magician, came on a visit to Ata's house. Ata was, of course, very much surprised to see him, for he had never before paid him a visit.

However, Oke talked very pleasantly, and noticed with delight that the grey parrot was still in the house, watching him with its bright, beady eyes.

"What a beautiful parrot you have!" exclaimed the cunning Oke.

"Oh," replied Ata carelessly, "this is not my parrot, but a wild bird which flew in from the forest and which is so fond of me that he never leaves me."

"He must be an affectionate bird!" said Oke, throwing grains of corn to the parrot. "Have you found a cure for the King's malady?"

"No," said Ata hastily. "I do not think there is any cure, and I am not troubling about it."

Just at this moment the parrot, who had been listening, called out:

"Charm! charm! Herbs and flowers! Efo and monkey-root!"

Ata sprang to his feet in a rage, for the parrot had announced the names of the two herbs with which he hoped to cure the King.

"What! Does this parrot speak?" cried Oke in pretended astonishment. "What were the words he uttered?"

"He only talks nonsense," replied Ata, relieved that his rival had not heard the fateful words.

As soon as Oke left the house, Ata began to mix the herbs so that he could take them to the King early in the morning. But Oke did not wait for morning! He went straight away that very

Oke Pays a Visit to Ata. *Page 96.*

night to the palace, and when he was admitted to the presence
of the sick King, he made a low bow and said:

"Sire, I have discovered the remedy for your complaint. If
Your Majesty will drink a mixture composed of efo and monkey-
root, the cure will be certain!"

The King at once ordered these two herbs to be procured,
and the magician stewed them in a pot before the eyes of all the
Court, and gave the King some of the concoction to drink.

The power of the herbs was such that the King was immediately cured, and he sprang up from his bed feeling stronger than
ever.

Next morning, when the second magician arrived with many
little vials with which he meant to mystify the Court, he found
himself laughed at by everybody, including the King, who was
now in perfect health. To his consternation Ata learnt that his
rival Oke had cured the King many hours before and had gone
home with the reward.

"And how was the King cured?" asked poor Ata.

"By efo and monkey-root," was the reply.

Then Ata knew that the words of the grey parrot had betrayed
his secret, and he resolved to kill the bird when he reached the
house. But on his way home it struck him that it might some day
be useful to possess such a clever creature. So he spared the
bird's life, and took such care of his pet that the parrot, which
had belonged to Oke, now began to consider Ata as its master
and to obey and understand him.

Some time later the King again sent for the two magicians,
and informed them that a gold chain which he prized very much
had been stolen from the palace by a large ape and carried away
into the forest.

"To anyone who finds out where my gold chain has been hidden, and who also tells me how it may be recovered," said the
King, "I will give a reward not to be despised even by a rich man!"

"Ah," said Oke, laughing, "that should not be difficult for me,
because I know all the secrets of the animals."

"Indeed," said Ata, smiling also, though he felt far from confident, "it will be an easy matter to discover the secret by means
of my charms."

And both magicians hastened away—Oke to solve the mystery in the depths of the forest, and Ata to sit at home and think how certain it was that his rival would win the reward, for he himself knew nothing about the creatures of the forest.

"I am a very unlucky man," he told his parrot sadly. "I lost the first reward through your talkativeness, and now my own ignorance will prevent me from winning the second!"

"Send me!" replied the grey parrot. "Send me! Send me!"

The magician stood up and danced for joy.

"I have it! I shall win this reward after all, and at last you can be of some use to me, you lazy bird! You betrayed me to Oke by your power of speech, and now in turn you must find out his secret for me. Fly away, my good pet, and listen hard to everything you hear at Oke's house."

Now when the grey parrot flew into Oke's house and perched on the shoulder of his old master, Oke was delighted and suspected nothing.

"Wicked bird!" he said playfully. "When I sent you to watch that false magician Ata so long ago, I did not think you would desert me! How happy I am to have you back again, and to know that Ata did not suspect you to be anything but a wild bird, which flew in to him from the forest! Ha! ha! ha! How well we have tricked him."

That evening when he was parching corn and ground-nuts, he gave the parrot all the biggest grains, and spent the time very happily with his old pet.

But the next afternoon, to his astonishment, Ata called to see him, with the excuse that he wished to know the remedy for a certain snake-bite.

Oke, who knew so much about animals, told him, but could not help feeling surprise that his rival should come to visit him after all their past disagreements.

Meanwhile Ata, who pretended not to see the grey parrot, began to talk about the reward offered by the King for his gold chain.

"There is little doubt," he said, "but that you will carry off this reward also, since you know so much about the forest. Have you discovered where the chain has been hidden by the ape who stole it from the palace?"

"No," said Oke hurriedly; "how should I know? I have nothing to do with this mystery."

But alas for his secret! The talkative grey parrot came sidling from a corner of the room, crying:

"Chain! Chain! Chain! King Ape's neck! Catch ape with chain-trap! Catch ape with chain-trap!"

Oke started violently, and was about to seize the bird and wring its neck, when Ata said, rubbing his hands with secret satisfaction:

"What language does your parrot speak? He talks in riddles! Do you understand him?"

"Indeed I do not!" replied Oke, leaning back in great relief at the denseness of his rival. "He talks sheer nonsense—some jabber-jabber he has learnt from the monkeys in the banana trees! He is the most foolish bird that ever came out of the forest."

Soon after this, Ata took his departure, and Oke resolved to go to the King that very evening and tell him what he had discovered.

But alas again for his secret! On leaving Oke's dwelling, the second magician set off to run as fast as he could to the palace, where he arrived quite out of breath and asked to be brought before the King.

"Oh, King!" he said, still panting—so anxious was he that Oke should not have the reward—"I have solved the mystery of your gold chain! The chain has been neither broken nor buried, and the King of the Apes, who loves bright things, wears it about his neck! I saw it gleaming as he climbed from branch to branch in the depths of the forest!"

"This is good news," said the King; "but how can we ever recover the chain? The King of the Apes is a fierce monster, and can defend himself against attack, while if he calls for help, the whole tribe of apes will descend and tear my hunters to pieces."

"To recover the chain," replied the magician modestly, "is a simple matter now that I have told you where to find it. All you have to do, is to conceal a trap on the ground; and in the trap you must place another gold chain. When the King of the Apes sees the gold shining, he will have no thought of danger, and will spring down into the trap to get the chain. It will then be an easy thing for your hunters to kill him and recover the stolen chain."

The King thought this an excellent idea, and hunters were sent at once to the forest to set the trap for the King of the Apes. Everything fell out as Ata had predicted from the words of the grey parrot. A few hours later the hunters returned in triumph with the monstrous body of the King Ape, wearing still the gold chain round his neck.

The King put on his chain and rejoiced, while Ata hurried away with the reward.

Immediately afterwards, the magician Oke arrived at the palace, requesting to see the King, and smiling mysteriously, as if he knew the inmost thoughts of both men and animals.

What was his consternation to see the King with the famous gold chain safely round his neck, and to hear that his rival, Ata, had gone off with the reward!

"And how was the chain recovered?" asked the unfortunate magician, and he was told:

"By setting a trap for the King of the Apes."

Then his wrath knew no bounds.

"My own parrot has given the secret away!" he exclaimed, rushing homewards in a fury. "I thought him clever and fed him with corn until he was as plump as a chicken, and he has served me this ungrateful trick! I will certainly wring his neck as soon as I reach home."

But the grey parrot was cleverer than his master thought. He flew away to the forest before Oke returned, and has never been seen since.

XXVI. Tortoise and the Cock

"Hard times indeed!" said Tortoise sadly, when his wife Nyanribo told him one evening that there was absolutely nothing for supper.

"Not even a little rice?" asked Tortoise plaintively.

"No," replied Nyanribo. "Not a taste of stew, not a grain of corn, not a single egg . . . and there is nothing for breakfast to-morrow. Ajapa, my poor husband, I am afraid we shall soon die of starvation!"

"No, indeed!" said Tortoise briskly. "That shall never happen while Tortoise has a shell on his back. I will find some means of obtaining food. Wait patiently at home for me, and all will be well."

With these words he set off to see what he could find. Near by was a farm, and in the farm-yard he could hear a hen clucking to inform all the other fowls that she had laid an egg.

Tortoise sighed. He was very fond of eggs, and so was Nyanribo, but the farmer and his daughter kept a close watch on the farm-yard, and it was impossible to remove any of the eggs without being seen by them.

Tortoise watched the Cock, with green-black feathers shining in the sun, walk proudly up and down among the hens, crowing now and again. Just then the farmer's daughter came out and chose a plump young fowl, which she carried into the house to be roasted for supper. The other hens and the Cock lamented the loss of this poor bird, and as they were complaining Tortoise stuck his head into the yard and said:

"Oh, but there is far worse to come!"

"Who are you, and what do you mean?" replied the Cock arrogantly.

"I am one who sees all that is going on," said Tortoise not untruthfully, "and I weep to think of what is about to happen to you."

The Cock and the hens crowded round Tortoise, fluttering, pecking, and clucking excitedly.

"Tell us what is to happen! What is to happen?"

"Now," began Tortoise gravely, looking at the Cock, "what happens if someone comes into the farm-yard in the night or early morning?"

"I crow as loudly as I can," said the Cock with pride, "and the farmer comes running out with a hunting-knife to defend his property."

"Ah!" said Tortoise wisely. "I thought as much. And what happens when dawn breaks?"

The Cock puffed out his chest, and his red comb and green-black feathers looked very handsome in the sunshine.

"At dawn," said the Cock solemnly, "I crow very loudly indeed, and keep on crowing until everybody is awake, and the farmer's daughter comes out to scatter grain for us and to collect the eggs."

"Ah!" said Tortoise again. "I thought as much! . . . Well, to-morrow morning you will crow for the last time."

The Cock's feathers rustled with fear.

"Alas! alas! How can that be? A moment ago the farmer's daughter carried off my favourite wife to a fate of which we do not care to think, and now you say that I am to follow her to-morrow!"

"Yes," said Tortoise. "I have been to the house, and I heard the farmer's daughter say that the first time you crow to-morrow shall be the signal for your death, as they intend to boil you for dinner."

"Oh! oh!" cried the poor Cock. "How terribly sad! And what an insult to boil me, as if I were not tender enough to roast! What can I do?"

"Well," replied Tortoise kindly, "I should advise you not to crow at all to-morrow, and then the farmer's daughter will have no signal, and you will not be thrown into the stew-pot."

The Cock thanked him very warmly and agreed not to crow at all. Then Tortoise went home, chuckling to himself, and had a sound sleep.

A little while before dawn, he left the house with a large basket and returned to the farm-yard. The Cock saw him, but was so afraid of the farmer's daughter that he dared not crow. Tortoise went softly to the nests of all the hens, collecting the eggs in his basket, until he could carry no more. Then he prepared to go home, saying to the foolish Cock as he went:

"Thank you! Your silence may not have saved you, but it has certainly saved me."

Long after the dawn, the farmer awoke, wondering why he had not heard the Cock crowing as usual. When the farmer's daughter went to collect the eggs, she was astonished too, for there were none!

"Alas!" said the farmer. "Something is wrong with our fowls. Perhaps they are starving. Scatter plenty of corn this morning, daughter!"

Now when the Cock saw the girl coming, he was filled with dread. She stretched out her hand, and he was sure that she meant to seize him in spite of his silence. But from her hand fell a golden shower of corn, and in his relief the Cock crowed loudly. To his amazement nothing happened, and he was so glad that he went on crowing for quite a long time.

The Cock crowed, and the hens laid eggs, and Tortoise and Nyanribo had a great feast and were very happy—only, of course, they never went near that farm-yard again!

XXVII. Tortoise Lets His House

Now Tortoise was such a spendthrift fellow that it was by no means unusual for him to be very hard up. The long-suffering Nyanribo made no complaint, even when money was very scarce indeed.

One day Tortoise stood in his doorway, looking out and wondering how to make a little money, when Mouse passed by in a great hurry with her seven children.

"Karo, Mouse!" said Tortoise. "How are you?"

"Oh dear!" gasped Mouse. "I am all in a flutter! What are we to do? The farmer has begun cutting down the grass in his field, and we are homeless! Oh, my poor children! Oh, what shall we do?"

"You will have to find another house," said Tortoise, thinking this might be a way of earning money. "How would you like to have my house?"

"This great mansion? Oh, dear me, no! All we need is a little cottage about the size of your shell . . . Now, how would you like to let us have your shell to live in?"

"Good gracious!" exclaimed poor Tortoise. "What should I do without it?"

"Your wife will take care of you," replied Mouse eagerly. "I will pay you a small bag of cowries every week for your shell, until we can find a proper house in one of the farmer's fields."

Tortoise was greatly tempted by the prospect of earning so much money in such a simple way, and at last he consented, and gave up his shell to Mouse and her family.

But when Nyanribo saw him without his shell she cried:

"Oh, how queer you look! I would never have married you if I thought you were such a flabby, feeble creature!"

"You would look exactly the same without your shell," protested her husband indignantly. "I have done this noble deed for your sake, and now you are ungrateful!"

Tortoise led a very miserable life in his shell-less condition. Everybody laughed at him, and to avoid them he stayed in the house all day and went out only at night. At the end of the week he asked Mouse for the payment she had promised.

"What rubbish is this about a promise?" said Mouse, looking contemptuously at him. "I'm sure I can make better use of the money than you could. Be off with you!"

"If you will not pay," said Tortoise, with as much dignity as possible, "you must find another house."

"Nothing of the sort! We are very comfortable here, and intend to stay as long as we like!"

And she went on with her task of making a cosy bed of dry grass for her seven children.

Tortoise sat at home lamenting his sad fate to Nyanribo.

"Here am I without a shell, the laughing-stock of everybody, and that wretched Mouse will not pay me a single cowrie! I am a very unlucky fellow!"

Thus matters went on from week to week.

"Go away, you queer-looking thing. I am busy cooking!" Mouse would say when he asked her for money. Or again:

"Go away, you hideous monster. Can't you see that my children are asleep?"

Tortoise at length decided that nothing but a trick would persuade Mouse to give up her abode. He stood one day outside his shell, near enough for Mouse to hear him, and called out to Nyanribo:

"Wife, let us go to the fields. The maize is nearly a foot high!"

"What!" cried Mouse, popping out her head. "Is the maize so high already? In that case I will go and find a nice new house in the field."

And off she went.

Tortoise made haste to push her seven lazy children out of the shell; they were big and fat and well able to look after themselves. Then Tortoise crept into his shell, and sighed with thankfulness.

Soon Mouse returned, indignant, having found that the corn was only a few inches high, and not tall enough to conceal a mouse from the farmer's sharp eyes. But Tortoise refused to come out again, though she promised him two bags of cowries a week for his shell.

"Go and live in an ant-hill!" said Tortoise rudely. "I know you will never pay me anything. There are plenty of empty houses—but mine will never be empty again!"

So Mouse collected her seven children together and set off to find another house, and from that day to this Tortoise has never been seen out of his shell.

XXVIII. The Monkeys and the Gorilla

> "Corn to eat,
> Life is sweet!
> Corn to eat,
> Life is sweet!"

sang Tortoise blithely, as he walked through the forest one fine, dry day, feeling very pleased with himself and the world in general.

He stopped singing rather suddenly, for there in front of him in the path stood the huge, hideous, hairy gorilla. The gorilla lived by himself in the forest, and everyone was afraid of him.

Tortoise was afraid like the rest, and his heart began to beat very fast when he saw him standing there so close to him.

"Karo!" said the gorilla, in a rough, deep voice.

"Karo!" said Tortoise nervously, wondering whether to turn back or go straight on under the gorilla's legs.

"You sound very happy," said the gorilla.

"Well," replied Tortoise more boldly, "it is a very beautiful day, and I like to sing when I am at peace with the world—but I am sorry indeed if my voice disturbed you."

"Certainly not!" said the gorilla. "To begin with, life has been very dull lately, since my wife got killed by a hunter, and in addition I am driven to distraction by the chattering of the monkeys. The wretched creatures seem to be on every branch of every tree, and no matter how deep into the forest I may go, I get no peace from them. I would like to crack all their heads together, but it would take me a whole rainy season, for they are so many!"

"Perhaps," Tortoise suggested timidly, "I can give them a hint that you would like a little silence now and then. . . ."

"A hint? Do you think those monkeys would take a hint?"

"Perhaps they would take a present instead," suggested Tortoise.

"Ah!" said the gorilla. "They might! Yes, that is a good idea. You can tell them that if they will stay at the edge of the forest, I will give them . . . I will give them . . ."

"Pineapples!" said Tortoise eagerly.

"Very well," returned the gruff gorilla. "I will give them pineapples, though I shall have to go far from my haunts to gather them."

Tortoise made haste to go in search of the monkeys. He found a whole family of them—uncles and cousins, babies and grandfathers, playing noisily in the banana trees.

After he had called to them for some time, they paused in their chattering and listened to him.

"I have just seen the gorilla," began Tortoise, but, with a cry of terror, the monkeys fled.

Tortoise patiently followed them, until he found them climbing about some more trees and swinging on the creepers. When they at last were quiet enough to hear him, he began again:

"The gorilla says . . ."

But with another shriek of fear and a lightning scramble of toes and tails, the monkeys left him far behind.

"Dear! dear! How tiresome!" grumbled Tortoise, as he went slowly after them. "They seem to be quite afraid of the gorilla."

This time he was more cautious and said:

"Please don't run away whenever I speak! What is the matter?"

"The gorilla," said all the monkeys together.

"Why, what is wrong with the gorilla?"

"Ugh! We fear him more than anything else in the forest. We know he is lying in wait all the time to eat us up."

"And he won't leave us in peace anywhere!" added an old grandfather monkey, in a very bad humour. "Wherever we go we come across him, and he makes our life miserable."

Now a very profitable plan came into Tortoise's head, and he replied: "Why don't you send the gorilla a present, and ask him

very politely to stay in his own part of the forest? I am sure he
would be glad to leave you alone."

The monkeys were very much excited and talked all at once,
but Tortoise made out that they agreed with his suggestion and
wished him to offer the gorilla a present.

"Good!" said Tortoise. "I am an obliging fellow, and quite will-
ing to help you. I think the gorilla would be pleased with a gift
of bananas! But I will ask him at once."

Tortoise briskly returned to the gorilla and told him that the
monkeys had agreed to keep silent for half the day if he gave them
twelve large pineapples. Feeling very pleased, the gorilla swung
away through the branches to the edge of the forest and brought
back twelve choice pineapples from a field. Tortoise at once hid
them in a hollow at the foot of a tree and went back to the monkeys, who were waiting for him with a great many questions.

Tortoise told them that he had found the gorilla in a very savage mood, but that in the end their enemy had agreed not to
molest them if they would give him a dozen large bunches of
bananas.

In a twinkling Tortoise found himself with a large stock of
bananas in addition to his pineapples, and as he had a good store
of provisions at home just then, he left all the fruit in the hollow
at the foot of the tree, and went away, singing cheerfully:

> "Fruit to eat,
>   Life is sweet!
> Fruit to eat,
>   Life is sweet!"

And there perhaps the story would have ended, but for one
inquisitive monkey who went poking about among the trees the
next day, and suddenly came across Tortoise's hiding-place. He
called the other monkeys to come and see.

"Why," exclaimed the old grandfather monkey, "here are our
bananas! And what are all these pineapples doing here? Tortoise
is up to some trick, I am sure."

Just then he saw the gorilla swinging from tree to tree, with
his mighty arms. With his heart beating very fast the grandfather
monkey called out:

"Lord Gorilla! Mighty Gorilla!"

The gorilla looked very fiercely down at him.

"Be off!" he growled. "After accepting my pineapples, you still come to torment me! I will devour you all. . . ."

"Oh, sir!" quavered the old monkey. "Your pineapples are hidden at the foot of this tree—and so are the bananas we sent you as a present yesterday!"

The gorilla was astonished and dropped down from his branch to peer into the hollow.

"My pineapples!" he said in a rage. "My twelve large pineapples!"

"And our twelve large bunches of bananas!" piped the monkeys in chorus.

After a very little discussion they realized the trick which Tortoise had played them.

"You may as well take the pineapples now that I have gathered them," said the gorilla graciously.

"And, of course, there is no sense in wasting these beautiful bananas, if you will kindly accept them. . . ."

Thus they parted quite amicably.

"But wait till I see Tortoise!" growled the gorilla, with his mouth full of banana. "I will crush his shell!"

And the monkeys, with their mouths full of pineapple, replied:

"We will tear him to bits—after you have crushed his shell!"

But this great catastrophe never happened, because all the time Tortoise had been sitting in the long grass near by, listening to them. When they had all gone away, he crept very softly home.

"Alas! My luscious pineapples! Alas! My sweet bananas!" he groaned.

But he was thankful at least that he had escaped without being crushed by the gorilla and torn to pieces by the monkeys.

When he was at a safe distance from the forest, he held up his head boldly and sang:

> "Fools to cheat,
> Life is sweet!
> Fools to cheat,
> Life is sweet!"

XXIX. The Wrestlers

Now in the country of which this story is related, wrestling is a national pastime, and in every village, in the cool of evening, the boys and young men may be seen locked together, swaying to and fro, testing the strength of their muscles.

Once upon a time the rumour spread that in a certain village there was a wrestler who had never known defeat—a small man, but very powerful, and no doubt wearing a secret charm which protected him against all his rivals.

The fame of this village wrestler grew, and came at length to the ears of the King, who, like his subjects, was passionately fond of the manliest of sports, though he himself, being a ruler, could only sit and applaud the struggles of others, whereas in secret he greatly longed to demonstrate his own prowess before an excited and cheering crowd.

"What is the name of this man?" he asked the messenger who had told him of the undefeated wrestler.

"His name, Your Majesty, is Lagbara."

"Well, then, I desire to see with my own eyes if Lagbara deserves his reputation. Send for the man, and let him be brought before me!"

Messengers were despatched with all haste to Lagbara's village, and in two days' time they brought the wrestler back with them to the palace.

But when the King saw the man about whom he had heard such wonders, he was struck not so much by the strength of his shoulders, as by the extreme ugliness of his features.

"Never," thought the King to himself, "have I seen such a

repulsive-looking man. Yet all the same it may be true that he is a good wrestler. I will try his powers."

The King's wrestlers were sent for, and Lagbara overthrew them one after another. As his favourites were carried away by the slaves, the King had to admit that the ugly man was certainly a terrible opponent; but the curious thing was that in every case the match was over in a few moments. On approaching Lagbara, each wrestler seemed to become paralyzed and was at once overthrown.

The King complimented the stranger on his strength, for no one had overthrown the royal wrestlers before.

"This is but child's play, Sire!" exclaimed Lagbara. "I can with ease overthrow a giant eight feet tall."

"We will see!" said the King. "There is such a man in my Court—a warrior of great renown. If you can overthrow him, I will give you any reward you ask."

The Court was thrown into a state of great excitement when the news was made known, and from far and wide people flocked to see the wrestling-match between Lagbara, the stranger, and Ogunro, the giant warrior.

The day and the hour at length arrived, and before the eyes of a great assembly Lagbara walked calmly into the circle which had been drawn on the ground. From the other side came Ogunro, the giant, staring with contempt at his small opponent.

The signal was given, and the two ran together; but as soon as they were face to face, Ogunro appeared transfixed with terror. He stood motionless, and in a few moments lay stretched out on the ground with his neck broken.

The crowd was silent with astonishment, and then broke into mighty shouts:

"Long live Lagbara! Hail the undefeated wrestler, the breaker of giants! Hail the King's champion!"

The King, robed in purple cloth and seated under the royal white umbrella, then asked Lagbara what reward he claimed for his victory.

The stranger bowed low, and smiled, looking fiercer and uglier than ever, as he replied:

"Sire, I claim the hand of your youngest daughter, the beautiful Princess Lewa, in marriage."

The young princess, who was present at the contest with her sisters, gave a shriek of horror, and even the King could not help shuddering, so repulsive was the appearance of the wrestler.

"Indeed," said the King, "you claim a very great reward! I have been searching four years to find a chief worthy to be the husband of Princess Lewa! However . . . I gave you my promise, and cannot turn your request aside. To-morrow evening I will give you my answer."

The wrestler bowed low and withdrew, the crowd melted away, and the King and his Court went into the palace. Here the beautiful princess flung herself at her father's feet, and declared with tears that she would rather die than marry a common wrestler from a remote village, and one who was, moreover, absolutely hideous to look upon.

"My daughter," replied the King sadly, "a royal promise cannot be broken. However, I will try to postpone the marriage by making a condition impossible for this wrestler to fulfil."

The King retired to his private apartment, and thought and thought, but for a long time he could not think how to delay the marriage. At last an idea came to him, and he issued a royal proclamation to Lagbara and also to the whole of the kingdom, that Lagbara should only marry the princess when he had overthrown the first six wrestlers who might offer to stand against him; and that if, by chance, Lagbara himself was overthrown in any of the contests, his victor should wed the princess.

When this proclamation had been beaten out by all the drummers, and passed from mouth to mouth throughout the town, the King rubbed his hands and felt happy again.

"For of course," he said to himself, "after seeing my giant Ogunro thrown by this ugly wrestler, no other man will dare to challenge him, and he will spend his life waiting in vain for the six opponents. Thus he can never marry my daughter."

But the King was mistaken.

The beauty of the Princess Lewa was such that it was not long before a bold young man challenged Lagbara in the hope of winning the princess as his wife. Alas for his hopes! He met the same fate as the others, and was carried groaning from the circle.

"Five more to defeat!" said Lagbara triumphantly, casting a look of admiration on the beautiful princess, who was so closely concerned with the result of the contest that she could not keep away, but had watched the match with her sisters.

When Lagbara fixed his eyes upon her, she met his look proudly, and at once fainted, to the consternation of those about her. She opened her eyes at last to find herself lying on a divan in her chamber, and immediately burst into tears.

All she could say was, that the glance of Lagbara had pierced her like a sharp spear, and caused her to faint with pain and terror.

"Sister," said one of the older princesses, "this must be the secret of Lagbara's victories—as soon as he fixes his eyes on his opponents, they are struck by the same emotion which you have described, and in that instant he overcomes them."

This indeed was the case, for a magician had poured into Lagbara's eyes a powerful charm which transfixed his enemies and so made it impossible for him to be defeated.

Princess Lewa now wept more bitterly than ever, for it seemed clear that if six youths were bold enough to challenge the strange wrestler, she could not escape from becoming his bride.

A second contest was soon ended, and the next week a third and fourth.

"Two more to defeat!" cried Lagbara joyfully, at the end of the fourth contest, looking again at his unwilling bride. But this time Lewa kept her eyes lowered, for she was afraid to meet his terrible glance, and only hoped that no one else would now be foolish enough to challenge her suitor.

The next day, however, there arrived at the palace a handsome young Chief named Oloto—a renowned wrestler in spite of his noble birth—to challenge Lagbara.

This young man sat in the shadow and covered his face with a gold-embroidered cloth, answering few questions; but from the door of her apartment Princess Lewa saw him enter, and fell at once deeply in love with him.

When she learned that the noble youth had travelled a long distance with the intention of challenging Lagbara to wrestle with him, she was filled with sadness, knowing how quickly he would be overthrown and perhaps killed.

Out of her love for Oloto she secretly sent messengers to him, entreating him to withdraw from the contest, and to leave the town at once; but the young Chief sent no reply, and when the fifth combat was proclaimed and the hour drew near, she grew almost frantic with grief, and wished to end her life before Oloto should have lost his own on her account.

The circle was drawn, and in the great courtyard a crowd gathered to behold the contest. The King sat under his white umbrella, attended by slaves with woven fans, looking gloomy and ill-humoured, and Princess Lewa herself stood in the background with her sisters, afraid to watch and yet unable to turn away her eyes.

Oloto was led to the edge of the circle, where he threw off his gold-embroidered cloth and stepped boldly forward, calling out the words of his challenge.

Then from the other side Lagbara sprang to face him, casting on him a death-dealing glance; but, without appearing to see it, Oloto seized him in a mighty grasp, and in a few moments Lagbara the undefeated lay helpless and groaning on the earth.

A great cry of exultation went up from the crowd, and the King's warriors shook their spears for joy. The King sprang to his feet and cried:

"Well done! Well done! My daughter is saved."

And Princess Lewa stepped shyly forward and held out her hand to the handsome Chief. But to the astonishment of all, Oloto stood still in the middle of the circle, and then turned slowly round, saying sadly:

"Beautiful Princess, whom I have never seen—where are you?"

"I am here, noble Chief," said Lewa softly. "Why do you not look at me?"

"Alas!" replied Oloto. "Because I am blind."

Then the princess understood how her lover had been victorious; since he was blind, the malignant glance of Lagbara had no effect upon him, and for the first time strength had decided the combat.

Smiling, Lewa went up to the young Chief and took his hand in betrothal.

"I love you, not in spite of, but actually because of, your blindness!" she declared, and seeing what a noble couple stood before them, the people cheered again, the King smiled radiantly, and the marriage was speedily celebrated with great pomp and splendour.

XXX. Why Tortoise Is Bald

Tortoise lay peacefully sleeping in his house during the heat of the day, not in the least suspecting that the animals were at that moment holding a secret conference under a wide-spreading iroko tree in the depths of the forest.

Leopard, who had called them all together, went through the names of the forest-dwellers, and the inhabitants of the marsh, and the denizens of the sea-shore, to make sure that nobody was missing.

"All here but Ajapa the Tortoise!" said Leopard with satisfaction. "That is as it should be."

A murmur of agreement went up from the assembled animals.

"Kindly hasten with the business," hissed the Python; "I have arranged a hunting expedition for this afternoon, and the hour of repose will soon be past."

"Undue haste! Undue haste!" growled the Leopard reprovingly. "This is a serious matter. I have received complaints from a great many of you about the tricks which Tortoise has played—sometimes maliciously, though more often from his misguided sense of humour, and it is clearly time that he was taught to mind his own business."

Everyone agreed with this except Pigeon, who timidly put in a good word for his friend; but the others drowned his voice and seemed very anxious to pay Tortoise back for the tricks he had served them.

"At least," pleaded Pigeon, "treat him gently, for I cannot consent to any plan which brings him real misfortune."

"Our plan will simply be to cover him with ridicule on account of his prying curiosity," replied Leopard.

For a long time the animals discussed how to cure Tortoise of his fault, and at last it was decided that they should all take it in turn to stand on guard outside an empty hut. Tortoise would be sure to think that there was something strange happening, or something of value hidden in the hut. When he had gone inside to look, the sentry was to give a signal, at which all the rest would suddenly appear and mock Tortoise for his curiosity until he was thoroughly ashamed.

Even Pigeon could see no harm in this mild joke, and he consented to be the first sentry on guard outside the hut.

When Tortoise awoke from his noontide sleep, he went out for a stroll, and discovered his friend Pigeon standing at the entrance to a near-by hut.

"Good-afternoon!" said Tortoise politely.

"Good-afternoon!" returned Pigeon, looking as mysterious as possible.

Tortoise opened his mouth to ask what his friend was doing outside the hut, but on second thoughts he felt that this would be impolite, as Pigeon had not offered to tell him, and so he continued his stroll and did not even peep into the hut.

After some time the first sentry was relieved by Wolf, who sat down looking very fierce, with his tongue hanging out of his mouth. At length Tortoise passed by, on his way homewards; but he was hungry and could smell his supper cooking, and besides, Wolf appeared so very fierce that Tortoise did not pause at all, but went straight into his house.

Now the Wolf was relieved by Lizard, a foolish animal, who stood waving his head from side to side until Tortoise came out to see if it was a fine night, and if Pigeon or any other of his friends was about.

When he saw still another sentry at the entrance of the hut, he began to think there was something in the air. He approached Lizard and said:

"What keeps you standing outside this hut?"

"I am on guard," said Lizard.

"Oh, so there is a prisoner in the hut?"

"No, indeed," replied the foolish sentry. "There is no one in the hut."

"Well then, there is perhaps treasure hidden here?"

"No," said Lizard, "the hut is quite empty."

Tortoise began to laugh.

"That is strange, to be sure! I have seen Pigeon and Wolf and now Lizard standing on guard—outside a hut which is quite empty! What is the meaning of this riddle?"

"Ah!" said Lizard wisely, "we are hoping to trap someone in the hut."

"Dear me!" returned Tortoise. "At least you will not trap me!"

And he went straight home to bed.

The animals met together during the night and were forced to admit that their plot had fallen through, but the Leopard had already thought of a better one.

"Opposite Tortoise's dwelling," he explained, "there is an empty hut with a large window. I will creep into the hut as softly as possible, and the rest of you must come one at a time to the window, reciting a line which we must compose beforehand; each time the line is recited, I will throw down some object of no value, concealed in a large leaf. Tortoise will be sure to hear what is going on, and in the hope of receiving a present from the person in the house, he will stand under the window and recite like the rest. But instead of a present, I will give him a bowl of cold water, which will cure him of his inquisitiveness for ever."

Everyone laughed heartily at this plan, but Squirrel, who had an old grudge against Tortoise, eagerly demanded to be the one inside the house.

"Well," said Leopard generously, "if you are so anxious to pour cold water over Tortoise's head, I don't mind letting you take my place. Do the rest agree?"

The animals all agreed, and began composing a line to recite outside the window.

Tortoise was snoring blissfully in his house, when a voice outside suddenly began to sing:

"If you have the treasure near,
Throw it down, the friend is here!"

Tortoise lost no time in going to his door, and was just able to see an exciting-looking parcel drop from the window opposite. The Wolf, who was standing below, picked it up and ran off into the forest.

"The animals have all gone mad!" said Tortoise. "It is a great nuisance, and to-morrow I will stick up a notice: 'Silence please!' on that house—perhaps they will learn not to disturb me when I am asleep!"

He was just going to sleep again, when another voice sang:

> "You who guard the treasure here,
> Throw it down, the friend is near!"

"Almost the same words as before!" thought Tortoise, peeping out to see another parcel drop into the paws of Leopard, who ran off quickly into the forest.

Tortoise watched for a while, and soon saw the Gorilla come up to the window, recite the same message, and receive a parcel in the same manner. Now Tortoise became very anxious to know who was in the house and what the mysterious parcels contained.

When Elephant had also gone by, Tortoise slipped out of his house and stood under the window opposite, singing in his squeaky voice:

> "If you have the treasure near,
> Throw it down, the friend is here!"

But alas! The spiteful Squirrel had prepared not cold but boiling water, and this he emptied on to the head of the unfortunate Tortoise.

Hearing cries of pain, the animals all came running out of the forest, to find their victim in a truly pitiable condition, while Squirrel made haste to disappear and was soon at the top of the tallest tree he could find.

"Alas!" said the Leopard in distress. "This is the result of your curiosity!"

"My curiosity was a natural one," replied poor Tortoise bitterly, "but my misfortune is the result of malice, and you have indeed played me a very cruel trick!"

The animals protested that Squirrel had altered their plan to suit his own malicious purpose.

"Indeed, Tortoise," declared the Crocodile, who had a tender heart and who shed large, fat tears on the ground as she spoke, "we meant to cure you of your curiosity, but how could we suspect that such a misfortune would befall you?"

Tortoise groaned in reply:

"Your regret may be sincere, but the deed is done, and I shall always be reminded of it when I think of my poor head."

And this was true, for ever afterwards Tortoise was bald, and remains so to this day, while Squirrel, his old enemy, keeps well out of reach and scolds him for his inquisitiveness from the branches of the trees.